THE INSOMNIAC

MIRANDA RIJKS

INKUBATOR
BOOKS

Published by Inkubator Books
www.inkubatorbooks.com

ISBN (eBook): 978-1-915275-80-6
ISBN (Paperback): 978-1-915275-81-3
ISBN (Hardback): 978-1-915275-82-0

Miranda Rijks has asserted her right to be identified as the author of this work.

THE INSOMNIAC is a work of fiction. People, places, events, and situations are the product of the author's imagination. Any resemblance to actual persons, living or dead is entirely coincidental.

PROLOGUE
THEN

I can't sleep. I try to get comfortable in bed but it's impossible, despite shifting into every conceivable position. It's my mind that's stopping me from relaxing, the racing thoughts and the fear that my life is about to come tumbling down. I made a mistake. A terrible mistake that could destroy everything I've worked so hard for. It was stupid and I should never have done it, never have strayed from what I know is right. But I did it and now they're going to make me pay.

Next week I have to go to the police station for an interview. They say that it's unofficial, but it's never unofficial if you're summoned, is it? They're suspicious and rightly so. I keep thinking about what I should say, whether I should tell the truth? But if I do, what then? It'll be all over either way.

I glance at the clock: 2:04 am. And then I hear a noise outside.

What was that? I sit up in bed and strain my ears. It's never totally quiet here because this is London and there's always a passing car or a distant siren. But that was a metallic clatter – at least I think it was.

I get out of bed and tiptoe towards the window, pulling the curtain back just a fraction. I think I see movement, a shadow to the side of my parked car. I let the curtain fall back and grab my phone, hurrying out of the room and down the stairs. An orange glow from the street lamp outside shines through the small window in the front door, bathing the hallway in a strange amber light. I hesitate for a moment and then double back to my small kitchen, where I grab a carving knife from the wooden knife block. It's a deterrent, one I hope I won't need.

I edge to the front door, slipping the chain off and turning the lock, waiting a moment and listening. The only sound is my laboured breathing. Perhaps this is a bad idea, standing here, barefoot and dressed in my pyjamas, but I open the door just a fraction.

'Who's there?'

I see a shadow move and a person comes into view just to the side of my silver car, right next to the green wheelie bin.

'I've called the police!' I lie, because the last thing I need is unnecessary contact with the police, not while I'm a person of interest.

But then headlights swing into the street, lighting up the pavement, and whoever it is runs. All I can make out is a person dressed fully in black, a beanie on his or her head, running at full pelt in the opposite direction to the car, which, as it comes into view, is a black London cab with its taxi light illuminated. Then there's silence. The cab indicates and turns left at the end of the street and the burglar has disappeared in the opposite direction. As if I haven't got enough to worry about.

The street descends into silence once more, curtains pulled across all upstairs windows. I walk back into the house, double lock and bolt the front door, and then I walk into every room of the house, double checking the windows are shut and the back door is also locked and bolted. The only sound is my heavy breathing. I pad back upstairs.

That little interlude hasn't made sleep any easier. Perhaps I should just give up and watch television but I don't. I lie there, then toss and turn.

When my alarm goes off at 5:30 am I'm jolted awake, so I must have fallen asleep at some point. My body aches but I force myself up and into the shower, getting ready for work, as I do every morning, remembering that I love my job, that I'm making a difference. For now, at least.

At 6:15 am, I'm out the front door, my back to the street as I lock up, because last night I was all alone in the house. Except for the prowler. And then I hear footsteps. I swivel around, the key still in the lock of the front door. There's a glint of metal.

'Get off me!' I say. But it's too late.

The blade is jabbed into the side of my neck and I know instantly it hit my jugular. I try to speak but no words come. I look into those terrifying, expressionless eyes and I can tell he has done what he set out to.

My knees give way and I sink to the ground. I won't be found for at least an hour because I leave for work earlier than anyone on this street. I try to shout out, but the sounds bubble up in my throat. I watch the knifeman walk away, a swagger to his step, as if he's accomplished what he set out to achieve. My last thought is, at least I won't need to go to the police interview. At least I'll be spared that indignity.

My eyes flutter closed as my head rolls back against the front door.

Blackness.

1

DAISY

Can't Sleep And Going Crazy

Public Group. 243K members. 10+ posts a day.

*If you find yourself here, the chances are you're like me —
an insomniac desperate to solve your sleeplessness. I can't
promise you solutions, but what I can offer you is a sense
of community. My name is Daisy McKenzie and I've been
an insomniac for over a decade. I'm still searching for solutions. I'm starting this Facebook group as a means of
therapy for myself and also to connect with other people in
the same boat. This is a continuation of my blog which
goes by the same name. Please introduce yourself, and if
you've got any great tips, do share with your fellow insomniacs. Please remember the rules: Be kind. Be courteous. No
insulting. No bullying. No bad language. No advertising.
No spamming. The admins' decisions are final.*

'Daisy, can you help me with the first sentence of my piece?'

I swallow my sigh. Isabella is a sweet girl, but how she got the position as intern at our magazine I have no idea. She has a propensity to write in text speak, and even then can barely string a sentence together. Perhaps her parents are friends with Garth, my editor.

'I'll email it to you,' she says. Isabella talks in a drawl, elongating the ends of words.

'You're never going to learn if you don't try it yourself,' I say a little too harshly. 'Write the whole article and then I'll review it.'

I keep my eyes glued to my screen, ignoring the stare from my colleague, Anika. She's a little older than me, in her early forties, but unlike me, she's happy to work here. For Anika, editing a monthly London magazine that consists mainly of reviews of new restaurants and boutiques along with the odd lifestyle piece, padded out with advertising and houses for sale, is her perfect job. She's a nine-to-five type of person, happy with her lot in life.

Me, not quite so much.

When I was Isabella's age, I had my career trajectory all planned out. After studying journalism, I was going to join a national newspaper, ideally a broadsheet. Then I would climb the greasy pole, doing serious investigative work, rooting out injustices, writing up compelling and sometimes controversial pieces, and getting my own byline. Forty seemed ancient back then. I was sure that after being a foreign correspondent I would be promoted to editor. For sure, I was going to be at the very top of the media tree.

Yet here I am, working on fluff pieces for a glossy magazine called *Live Life London*, earning a pittance. Things never work out the way we imagine when we're young.

'Garth wants to see you,' Samesh says, as he walks past my desk holding a large pile of folders. He stops and peers at me. 'Are you alright, Daisy?'

'Yes, thanks, just tired.'

He nods and carries on walking. Samesh works in accounts, or rather he *is* accounts. We're a small team here and every day I wonder if we're going to become smaller. My only hope is that if the powers that be want to cull staff, they're likely to go for last in first out, and as I've been employed for over eight years, I won't be the cheapest or easiest to get rid of.

I stifle a yawn and get up from my desk. I know I look awful. Even Millie, my eight-year-old, asked if I was ill when I ushered my son and daughter into the car this morning, and a kid shouldn't have to ask such a question.

I grab my handbag and pad of paper and dash to the toilets. I peer at my reflection in the mirror, barely recognising myself. The circles underneath my brown eyes are mauve and puffy. I have lines on my forehead and little wrinkles by my lips that I swear weren't there a few weeks ago.

It's the insomnia. It's always the insomnia.

I take out my concealer and dab it onto the circles under my eyes and then add another layer. I swipe some pink lipstick across my lips and pinch my cheeks. That will have to do. Even the best makeup can't hide my sleep deficit. I reckon I got two hours last night, three at a push, and that was a good night.

'Garth,' I say brightly, as I knock and immediately open the door of my boss's office. The rest of our small team sits in an open-plan room, our desks wedged up against each other, but Garth has his own space and he's very proud of it.

'Come in, Daisy, and shut the door behind you.'

I do as I'm told and sit in the chair opposite Garth's desk, my pad of paper balanced on my knee. Garth is late fifties with sallow skin, and balding. He pretends to be young and hip, wearing oversized, square tortoise-shell glasses and skinny jeans, ranting about the endless opportunities presented by social media. We all know he hasn't got a clue what he's talking about.

'This is a little follow-up to your performance review last month.'

My heart sinks. He rubs his hands together and glances out of the window. I brace because I know it's not going to be good news.

'The thing is, you've not really upped the ante, Daisy. You're forgetting stuff and I asked you to be proactive, to pitch new ideas, to come up with a column for Isabella to write and, well, I haven't seen anything. Also, I hope you don't mind me saying, and some of the others have also mentioned it, but maybe you're not very well. Not feeling yourself. Are you still suffering from insomnia?'

'Are you sacking me?'

Garth's eyes widen and his chin wobbles. 'Good heavens, no. I'm just worried about you, and you know the pressures we're all under.'

That means I've got a stay of execution, for now at least.

I relax slightly. 'I'm sorry, Garth. You're right, I'm exhausted. I just can't sleep or get the insomnia under control. There are a few stresses at home as well, which may have distracted me. I know that's not good enough.'

'Anything you'd like to share?' Garth asks, pulling his concerned face while shuffling uneasily in his chair.

'Haydn's new business is struggling a bit. Nothing too serious but I've probably let it get to me. We're rather reliant on my salary, you see.'

'If there's anything I can do to help...' His voice peters out, because we both know that Garth can't up my paltry salary. *Live Life London* is one small, unprofitable magazine owned by a large, media conglomeration, and even though Garth is the editor, he's just a puppet controlled by the powers higher up in the organisation.

'Maybe see the doctor,' he suggests. 'My wife swears by her sleeping pills. Just try to focus a bit on the work, because we're under a lot of financial pressure. I know you understand, Daisy.'

I nod because I do. This is a veiled threat. The trouble is, I'm not sure what I can do about it. I can't go back to my GP. She won't give me any more sleeping pills and I really don't want to take tranquillisers. My chronic sleep problem is something I need to grapple with alone. I've failed so far, but perhaps there are some tricks I've missed. I just need to stop worrying about my husband's new construction business and accept that the children will have issues at school from time to time.

When I move to stand up, Garth waves a sheet of paper at me. 'I've got something for you that will be right up your street. We've had an invitation to send a journalist to try out a new spa and sleep clinic. They're after a review and obviously you're the perfect person to go. Perhaps this place will be your cure.'

Garth hands me a press release and a fancy brochure printed on heavy, textured paper. It's headed *The Serinity Spa* in a fancy, cursive script.

'They're offering a week's stay, all expenses paid in return for a review.'

I raise my eyebrows. It's not like *Live Life London* is similar to *Good Housekeeping* or *Red Magazine* with a massive circulation and a healthy budget. I'm surprised that the spa is being so generous, but then again, we are read by London people with money. You'll find our magazine in Harley Street waiting rooms and shoved through the doors of luxury Mayfair and

Chelsea homes. I suppose our readers are the spa's perfect clientele.

'Go soon,' Garth says. 'I think you need it.'

'Thanks, Garth.'

I stand up, clutching the brochure and press release. I should be happy about this, excited for the opportunity, because everyone wants a freebie – especially something as big as this – but I'm not. That's the trouble with insomnia. It wraps you in a heavy armour that stops you from feeling, especially positive emotions. It makes you focus on the problems and the negativity.

I drag my weary body back to my desk and sit down heavily, only then realising the implications. How on earth can I go away for a whole week? It's absolutely impossible. I'm the person who takes the children to school in the mornings, who collects them from their after-school club, who makes sure we all have a meal on the table and clean clothes to wear. Haydn is under much too much pressure with his business to deal with the minutiae of our family life.

He set up McKenzie Makes Homes (yes – a cheesy name I know, but it's memorable) eighteen months ago. He's been unhappy for a long time, working as a site manager for a firm that builds large, residential estates on greenfield sites. If you drive past any middling-sized town in West Sussex, you'll see the sprawling, new housing developments. The homes Haydn built were largely identical with little innovative design, and he felt disillusioned by the lack of creativity and out-of-the-box thinking. He felt the pressure enormously, struggling to juggle the often unrealistic financial and time pressures piled upon him and his team by the money men at the top. Yes, he was earning well enough, but he's always dreamed of having his own building firm, a small business doing luxury renovations or upmarket, bespoke new builds.

It was me who told him to go for it. Just because one of us

hadn't realised our dreams didn't mean the other shouldn't. My salary is lousy but we reckoned we could make do for a year until he started to turn a profit. Perhaps we were naive, but it hasn't gone as well as he projected, and now we're struggling financially. It's my salary that pays the mortgage and the household bills, but it barely stretches to the weekly shop, and there's certainly not enough to buy new clothes or have a holiday. Our credit cards are maxed out too. Haydn hopes to win two new lucrative contracts shortly, and if he does, we'll be able to breathe again. If he doesn't... Well, I don't like to think about that.

I flick through The Serenity Spa brochure. The pages are thick and glossy and exude top-notch design and luxury. The place looks amazing in the photographs, showing big, white beds in neutral-toned rooms overlooking a startlingly blue sea. It's located on the south coast, but I'm pretty sure that sea has been photoshopped because I've never seen the English Channel looking that azure. Nevertheless, the spa looks great. Except, how can I go?

And how can I not go?

If I say no to Garth, there is zero doubt that I will lose my job. I probably won't even get a decent redundancy package because he's got enough to prove that I'm falling short of the standards expected of me. That's what all these assessments and not-so-casual chats have been about: creating a paper trail for human resources in our head office. I run my hands through my greasy hair and groan.

'What's up?' Anika asks.

'Garth wants me to go and stay in a new spa place but I'm worried about leaving Haydn and the kids for a whole week.'

Isabella appears at my desk, Her long, cerise cotton dress is so bright, it almost blinds me.

She picks up the brochure. 'OMG! You're going to The Serenity. Mummy's booked in there but not for months. It's fully booked up, apparently. It's run by Amity Augustiago. That's so cool. I'm well jell!'

'Jealous,' Anika mutters, although I'm getting used to Isabella's slang which sounds more weird when spoken in her posh, rounded accent.

'I'm only going because they're starting a new sleep clinic,' I say, holding up the press release.

'I'm happy for you,' Anika says. 'You need it.'

I place the brochure and press release on top of a large pile of paper on my in-tray to be dealt with at a later date.

IT ISN'T until Haydn is home and the children are upstairs that I have the chance to really think about the sleep clinic. I'm so conflicted. On one hand I'd love to go, as it would be great to have an instant fix and not feel this utter exhaustion all the time. On the other, I don't want to leave the kids, or be forced to do any kind of therapy. But I've clearly got no choice. I broach the subject with Haydn during our normal after-supper ritual when I wash up and he dries.

'That's great, Daisy,' he enthuses. 'It'll be fantastic if they can cure you.'

'Cure me? I very much doubt that will happen in a week.'

'Even if your insomnia improves just a little, it will be worthwhile,' Haydn says.

I know how worried he is about my insomnia; he tries not to show it because that just stresses me more. It impacts him too, not least because most nights I take myself off to the spare room to sleep and in the mornings I'm grumpy and uncommunicative.

'But I can't leave you for a whole week. How will you manage with the school runs and meals and everything?'

He puts the tea towel down on the drainer and pulls me

towards him. I hold my marigold-clad hands in the air to stop the soap suds from drenching us.

'This is exactly what you need and what you deserve, Daisy. You've held everything together for me and the kids and I'm really happy for you. Have a wonderful relaxing week and if you come back cured, how amazing would that be?' He places a kiss on the tip of my nose.

I briefly close my eyes and wonder what I did to deserve such a kind husband.

'I'll get Mum over. She can stay for the week,' he adds.

I wriggle out of his grasp.

That is exactly what I feared. Margot and I don't have the easiest of relationships. I know she judges me and finds me wanting. My house is never quite tidy or clean enough; the children's manners are lacking; I don't understand her son as well as she does. She has the passive-aggressive thing down to a tee because she's never blatant with these criticisms, either choosing her moment so that Haydn is out of earshot or commenting in a clever way so that Haydn simply misses his mother's cutting undertones. I suppose I'll just have to suck it up this time. At least she'll be here the whole week and should keep the children and the house safe. Or I hope she will, at least.

Haydn doesn't know the full extent of my sleeplessness. If he did, I doubt he'd let me drive let alone be the sole care-taker of the children. The thing is with insomnia, you learn to live with it. When I get up in the morning, I never feel as bad as I assume I'm going to while lying awake at 3 am, tossing and turning and listening to useless meditations through my AirPods. I try not to disturb Haydn whenever I'm annoyed by his steady breathing and decamp to the spare room. It's later in the day that it hits me, normally between 2 and 3 pm, when I'm at my desk in the office. That's when the worry sets in, which then churns into a panic as bedtime approaches. I'm so tired in the evening. No, tired isn't a good enough description. It feels as if my eyes are burning, my head is stuffed with absorbent towels that leech my coherent thoughts and my bones are made of iron. And yet I have to carry on. Even if I go to bed, which is what my body is screaming for, sleep won't come. Occasionally it does, but then I wake up an hour or so later, my heart thumping, adrenaline coursing through my veins, as if something terrible has just happened or is about to. After that, any hope of sleep is futile. This is nothing new; far from it. But it's getting worse.

Once we finish tidying up the kitchen and Haydn is installed in front of the television in the living room, I sit at the kitchen table, fire up my laptop and log onto my Facebook group's page, *Can't Sleep And Going Crazy*. I started writing an insomnia blog three years ago and when I got more and more feedback and followers, I added a Facebook group. Now I have an insanely large following, which is both reassuring and rather depressing to know how many other people are afflicted by sleeplessness. I started the blog as a way to keep a sleep diary (bad idea because that stressed me even more), and to document all the different anti-insomnia products and therapies that I half-heartedly tried over the years. These days I get sent free products to review, although I don't give honest feedback because I'm a lousy test case. If I think a product has a hope of working – or at least makes me feel a little sleepy and good – then I'll give it five stars.

I had to recruit a few other admins for the group because there's no way I can keep up with how much it has expanded. There are a heck of a lot of insomniacs out there and it's comforting, in a perverse sort of way, to know that we're all in this together. Of course, everyone comes to sleeplessness in their own unique way. For some it's driven by worry or nerves, for others it's trauma, ill health or pain; for others it's just a habit with no known cause, and for a growing number, it's a result of alcoholism or drug addiction of both the legal and illegal kind.

For me, sleeplessness is my penance. That's a truth I can barely admit to myself and will certainly never share with the group. It's my horrible little secret.

2

DAISY

Can't Sleep And Going Crazy

Public Group. 243K members. 10+ posts a day.

Daisy McKenzie
*Anyone been to a sleep clinic? I've been invited to attend a
sleep programme next week in return for writing an honest
review and would love to know what to expect!*

Tammy Shin
*Hubby sent me to The Worsterhouzer Clinic in Austria. It
was brutal. Don't recommend.*

Mindy Westerfield
*Relaxation treatments, sleep hygiene tuition, therapy.
Honestly Daisy, I think you already know it all. Hope you
have a lovely time anyways x*

Rosemary Burgh
Please tell us where you're going? Soooo exciting!

Tammy Shin
We'd all love to know.

Daisy McKenzie
The Serinity Spa is starting a new insomnia programme.
I'll be sure to report back!

Mindy Westerfield
Wow! Wow! You lucky girl! Heard amazing things about
The Serinity. Have fun xx

G arth is correct, I am forgetting things.
I have long lists of to-dos on my desk at work, on my laptop, my phone, pinned onto the fridge in the kitchen and in a little notebook next to my bed. Each day merges into the next, interspersed by hours of tossing and turning in bed and fretting about my lack of sleep. My life is all about firefighting, responding to the little crises that the children have at school, the bigger crisis that Haydn and I have when confronted with our weekly outgoings and the fact that I'm handing in my shoddily written articles one minute before deadlines. I am existing in a haze of exhaustion. Now, suddenly, the date for my biggest freebie so far is upon me and I'm in a total flap.

I am midway through writing an enormous list of everything that Margot needs to remember for the children when my mother-in-law herself arrives. Millie and Ollie race to say hello, eager to receive the gifts she always spoils them with.

'I don't smell anything cooking,' she says, as she strides into the kitchen wearing a Liberty print dress, her dyed auburn hair freshly blow-dried.

'I haven't had time to make supper yet,' I murmur.

'Thought I'd order a takeaway. What do you prefer, Chinese or Italian?'

'A takeaway!' Margot speaks as if it's a profanity.

'I've given the kids their tea and they're about to have a bath.'

'What did you have for tea?' she asks them.

'Fish fingers, chips and beans,' Ollie says breezily without realising the implications of the truth.

'Children, go upstairs and I'll be up to run your bath in a moment,' I say because I know exactly what's coming. At least Margot waits until we can hear their feet on the stairs before speaking. And then I brace myself.

'Daisy!' she exclaims, sitting down next to me at the kitchen table. 'I mean, really? How can you feed your children junk food? It explains why they're having problems at school. Nutrition lies at the very heart of successful child rearing.'

I clench my fingers into fists but I can't stop myself from retorting. 'I have been at work all day. I have no help from my husband and I am trying to prepare to go away for a week.'

'On a jolly by the sounds of it,' she says. 'You really don't appreciate how good you've got it. Haydn is the most wonderful husband.'

'It's a work secondment. Not all of us are lucky enough to be stay-at-home wives!' I say through gritted teeth, immediately regretting my words.

'Your children are more important than work–' And then I zone out because I hear Haydn's car pull up in the driveway and any moment now he's going to walk into the room.

'It's time you put them first,' Margot says.

Unfortunately, I hear that and it pushes me right over the edge. I stand up, shoving my chair backwards so it topples over. 'I am doing the bloody best I can!'

'Daisy!' Haydn is in the doorway. 'What's going on?'

'Nothing,' I mutter. I push past Haydn and storm up the stairs, angrily wiping the tears from my eyes. I know I shouldn't let Margot get to me, but she knows exactly which buttons to push and I rise to it every single time.

I'm undressing Ollie when Haydn comes into the bathroom. After giving their dad a hug, Haydn pops him and Millie in the bath and then takes my hand, tugging me out into the hall.

'What was all that about?' he asks.

'As normal, your mother is criticising me and my child-raising skills, and I'm sorry if I'm not good enough but I'm doing my absolute best.'

'Come here, darling,' he says, pulling me into a hug. 'I'm sorry about Mum.'

'I'm sorry I shouted,' I say, allowing myself to relax into his arms. I've always felt Haydn was too good looking for me with his short, curly dark-brown hair, big blue eyes and muscled torso.

'It's good that you're going away for a week. I mean we'll miss you terribly, but if your insomnia is cured, you'll feel so much better.'

'I don't want to go,' I murmur. 'I don't want to be without you or the kids.'

'We'll miss you but we'll be fine. This is a once-in-a-lifetime opportunity and you just need to enjoy it.'

'But your mother–'

'Will cope perfectly fine. She didn't do a bad job bringing up me and Craig.'

I grimace. 'I suppose not. But you will make sure that she doesn't open the door to strangers and she remembers to put the alarm on, even if she's just nipping to the shops? I've written her a comprehensive list but I might have forgotten something.'

'Hey, you.' Haydn puts a finger to my lips. 'You need to

stop worrying. Go downstairs, have a glass of wine and make up with Mum. I'll get the kids into bed.'

'But–'

Haydn clenches his jaw and that's the sign that I'm about to push him into an argument. It's what we always fight about – security, my fear that something bad will happen to Millie or Ollie, whether we should upgrade our alarm system, how safe their school is.

'Leave us your checklist and I'll make sure Mum follows it,' he says, before turning his back on me and walking into the bathroom.

THE SERINITY SPA is on the south coast between Little-hampton and Goring. The approach road is inauspicious, and I drive through endless roads of houses that get progressively larger and more desirable the closer I get to the seafront. Most of the properties are wedged quite closely together but perhaps that doesn't matter if you have the beach as your back garden.

The sign to The Serinity Spa is small and discrete, next to a large rock painted in white. I wonder what the neighbours around here thought about a spa opening on their doorstep; I assume they weren't too thrilled. A high, wooden fence extends along a much larger frontage than the adjacent properties and the entrance itself is hidden by electric gates. There is an intercom with flashing blue lights attached to a metal post. I lean out of my car window and press the button.

'Good morning, how can I help you?' the disembodied voice asks.

'It's Daisy McKenzie, here for a stay.'

The gate slides open to allow me in.

The building is huge and modern – austere even – with vast panels of glass, dark-grey steel struts and surrounds accompanying pale-grey rendered walls. Directly in front of me is a small, paved parking area. Two topiary bushes stand either side of the glass front door. As I switch off the engine, a young man steps out of the front door. He's wearing a crisp white shirt and navy trousers. Before I can open the car door, he does it for me and then nods deferentially, saying, 'Welcome to The Serinity Spa, Mrs McKenzie. My name is Tom and I hope you had a good journey.'

'Thank you,' I say, rather taken aback. I've never stayed anywhere smart enough for a doorman to open the car door.

'May I help you with your bags?'

'Sure, of course,' I say awkwardly, getting out of the car and walking around to the boot. I wish now I'd cleaned my VW Golf before driving down here. He takes my suitcase out of the boot and fortunately doesn't bat an eyelid at the mess.

'If I could have your car keys, I'll park your car in the basement garage.'

I try not to show my hesitation when handing over my keys, reassuring myself that the spa will be insured if anything happens.

Tom locks my car remotely and then leads me through the open front door into the lobby. Everything is white. The floor is white marble and the walls are painted white. There is a circular glass console table directly in front of me with a huge display of scented, white lilies in a globular white bowl. To the right is another glass table, which I assume must be the reception desk, because a young woman with blonde hair tied back in a ponytail is seated there, in front of a large iMac. Behind her is a closed door and a couple of verdant palm trees several feet high. She jumps up as soon as she sees me and I note that she's also wearing a crisp white shirt and navy trousers.

'Good morning, Mrs McKenzie. I'm Jenny and Amity Augustiago, the owner, will be along shortly to welcome you.'

I gaze through the hallway to the huge, open-plan lounge beyond where massive glass sliding doors allow a view straight to the sea, which is surprisingly blue today. There are multiple, sleek modern sofas and chairs all in creams and taupes, piled high with cushions. Long-piled rugs in cream soften the pale wooden floor. A cluster of wicker hanging chairs are suspended from the ceiling near a roaring fire in one of those fancy, glass stove boxes with a view out every side. There are large bouquets of white lilies in vases on side tables and the air smells of lilies and fresh linen. This place is stunning.

'Wow!' I say as I step into the lounge.

The right-hand side of the living room gives way to a dining room with five small tables. Each table is covered in a starched white tablecloth and a single white flower sits in a globular glass vase. A variety of seascapes hang on the walls in the living room while monochrome botanical prints adorn the dining room. I have never stood in such a place of tranquillity and luxury.

I remove my mobile phone from my handbag to snap some pictures, to share on *Can't Sleep And Going Crazy* when I get home. I jump when someone taps me on my shoulder and swivel around, surprised that I didn't hear any footsteps. I come face to face with Amity herself. I only know it's her because her photo is on the first page of The Serinity Spa's glossy brochure.

'Daisy, I presume?' Amity says in a quiet but deep voice, with a hint of a mid-Atlantic accent. 'I'm very sorry, but we have a no-phone policy here.'

'Oh,' I say, 'I didn't realise.' I shove my phone back into my handbag, wondering how I'm going to cope without it. Perhaps it's only disallowed in public places which makes a lot of sense.

'Sorry that a rule is my first introduction,' she says with a bashful smile. 'Welcome to The Serenity Spa. I'm Amity and it's my absolute pleasure to welcome you here. I'm very excited to help you on your journey to wonderful, restorative sleep.'

'Thank you,' I say. 'I'm very grateful to be offered the experience.'

Amity is beautiful, with long, flowing black hair that is both glossy and wavy and looks as if it should be in a shampoo advert. She has golden skin and dark, almond-shaped eyes, and other than a line of kohl around her lashes, her face is makeup free. Her lips are thin, her teeth straight and almost fluorescent white. She's wearing a cream linen dress that hangs loosely over her slender frame and her feet are in wedged, open toe sandals, her toe nails painted in pale pink.

'Please have a seat, Daisy, and I'll talk you through how everything works here. But first, if you don't mind, I need to take your phone and any iPad or laptop you might have brought with you. This comes as a bit of a shock for many of our guests but we are very serious about everyone having a digital detox whilst they stay here. We've done everything we can to mitigate electromagnetic hypersensitivity. We don't have any electronic devices or Wi-Fi anywhere except in the office and at the reception desk. In the bedrooms, all of the undersheets are shot through with silver and copper threads to negate any residual electromagnetic fields.'

'Oh,' I say, not really understanding what she just said. I'm sure that various people have talked about electromagnetic fields on the Facebook group but I tend to ignore the more hardcore insomnia solutions. 'Will I be able to speak to my kids and husband and check in with work?'

Amity shakes her head, her silken hair swaying like a curtain. 'I'm sorry, Daisy, but if we're going to cure you of your sleeplessness you need a total cut-off from the outside world.

Please rest assured that we will pass on any urgent messages to you from home.'

'But what about photos for the article?' I ask, desperately seeking a reason for my phone to stay with me.

'I'll forward you lots of lovely photos when you're back at work. We have a batch taken professionally for media use.' She holds out one hand, her palm upwards.Very reluctantly I switch off my phone and hand it over. 'Don't worry, we'll take good care of it. It will be locked away in my office. And do you have any iPad or laptop in your luggage?'

I nod and remove my laptop from my large shoulder bag. This time I'm even more reluctant as it includes all of my work and access to *Can't Sleep And Going Crazy*. I reassure myself that the laptop is password protected.

'Please rest assured, all electronic devices are very safe and won't be touched.'

I smile tightly but I'm not comfortable. Not at all.

3

DAISY

Clutching my phone and laptop, Amity turns and strides towards the hallway where she disappears through the door behind the glass reception desk. I take a moment to gaze at the sea and then walk right up to the patio doors. I notice a large decking area below with a cerulean infinity swimming pool, with water that flickers as if we were in the Mediterranean. Although it's sunny Sussex by the sea, it's still only May, so unless it's very well heated, I doubt anyone will be using the pool any time soon. I walk back into the heart of the lounge and sit on a soft, feather-filled sofa.

Amity returns to me accompanied by Jenny, the girl on reception, who is holding a little silver tray with a glass filled with a putrid-looking green juice. She places the juice on the pale-oak coffee table in front of me.

'Enjoy,' Jenny says and walks quickly away.

I'm not a fan of juices and particularly not the green variety, being quite happy to consume my vegetables the normal way. Fortunately Amity doesn't seem to expect me to drink it immediately, and instead hands me a pen covered in burnished wood with the word *Serinity* engraved on the side and a clipboard with several sheets of paper attached.

'Please can you have a read through these and sign in the various places that are marked up. These pages include our terms and conditions, our privacy policy, which is very important because we take every precaution to preserve the anonymity of our guests and their confidential details, and a disclaimer form. There is also a questionnaire regarding your personal likes and dislikes, including foods, and a pillow menu. Apologies for giving you so much paperwork but it's really helpful to get all of this out of the way first.' Amity smiles widely. 'Take as long as you need and when you're done, I'll show you to your room and around the spa.'

Amity is right. There is a crazy amount of paperwork.

I start with the terms and conditions and disclaimer form, which are full of legalese – sentences that extend for paragraphs without any punctuation. After reading the first page, I give up and skim through the rest. From what I understand, I'm basically signing away any right to sue The Serinity Spa should their treatments fail to deliver. I suppose it's standard practice to ask high-paying guests not to take legal action after their stay, but as I'm not a high-paying guest, it's not very relevant to me.

I sign both.

The personal questionnaire is of more interest, reminding me of a psychometric test but skewed towards my sleep habits. I have to state what time I go to bed, how long it takes me to fall asleep, what my dreams are like, what level of sleep hygiene I follow – i.e. sleeping without light, noise, on a new mattress, whether I'm disturbed by my partner and whether I do anything in the bedroom other than sleep or sex. It's personal stuff and my sweaty fingers struggle to grip the pen. I also answer questions on my health, ticking the not applicable boxes next to medication and major health problems, of which fortunately I've had few other than this wretched insomnia. Then I have to list my favourite and least favourite foods. The questions on food bodes well.

The form filling takes almost half an hour and the green juice is still untouched on the coffee table when I finish. I lift it to my lips and drink it as quickly as I can. Actually it's not as vile as I expected. I stand up and walk towards the reception desk, where Jenny is seated. I hand her the forms and then, almost instantly, Amity appears from the office, quickly closing the door behind her so I can't glance inside.

'Tom has already taken your luggage to your room, so would you like to see it?'

'Of course,' I say.

I follow Amity through a corridor leading off the entrance hall.

'We only have a handful of rooms here,' she says, talking over her shoulder. 'It's a very intimate spa, because we offer totally personalised treatment plans and also maintain the anonymity of our guests. Obviously I can't name names, but last week we had a prime minister's wife staying, a Hollywood A lister and a Nobel Peace Prize winner. The week before we welcomed two members of different royal families.'

Amity pulls her shoulders back as she says this, and although she's obviously very proud of her successful clientele, it doesn't impress me. I may only be a fluff journalist these days, but I'm perfectly aware that even the most successful, high profile people are just like you or me, simply paddling faster to keep their heads above water. I'm sure they paid a fortune to stay here, whereas I'm here for free. I reckon I've got the upper hand on that one.

Amity comes to a halt outside a door that has a name plate with *Repose* on it.

'We've named our client suites after synonyms of serenity, such as Peace, Repose, Tranquillity, Respite and Calm. I chose Repose for you.' She removes a key card from the pocket of her linen dress and swipes it in front of the keypad, then hands it to me. After opening the door, she uses her arm to keep it propped back and beckons for me to walk in.

It's a huge room, with a super king-sized bed made up with bright white linen. The walls are covered in a textured, pale-cream wallpaper and heavy beige curtains frame the spectacular rectangle window that gives a wide vista of the shimmering sea. I'm drawn towards the view and as I stand there, I see the infinity pool down to my left. A tall, wooden fence dissects a strip of grass directly in front of the building and the grass gives way to the pebbly beach and the English Channel beyond.

'This is gorgeous,' I murmur.

'Thank you,' Amity says, silently padding over to my side. 'There are blackout blinds which I strongly recommend you pull down before going to sleep. We'll select pillows and a duvet for you based on your questionnaire. The goose down pillows and lightweight goose down duvet already on the bed come as standard. However there's also a weighted blanket in the cupboard, which might be useful for you to try. It's excellent for people with sensory overload and can provide a calming effect. We'll talk about that in our sessions. The sheets are the finest Egyptian linen with one thousand thread count. The bathroom is through there.'

Amity paces towards a door and opens it to reveal a white marble bathroom with a rain shower and a separate bath. 'I've left you some delicious bath oils, predominantly lavender, geranium and frankincense, all ideal for helping you sleep. How about I pop back in twenty minutes once you've had the chance to freshen up after your journey? And then I'll show you around the rest of the spa. Please remove your clothes which the team will launder. We like our guests to wear our bathrobes during their stay here as it's more relaxing and anonymising. Leave your underwear or swimwear on underneath. The bathrobe is hanging up in your wardrobe and you'll be given a fresh one twice a day, or more on request.'

And then she's gone, leaving behind the scent of patchouli perfume. I sink onto the bed and it's so soft, it's difficult to get back up from it. I unpack my things, placing my clothes in the built-in wardrobe on the wall facing the window and put my washbag in the bathroom. I strip off and pull on the thick, fluffy white bathrobe and then sit down on the bed again. Although this room is lovely, it isn't until now that I realise how bare it is. There is no television, no phone, no books. There aren't even any pictures on the walls. I suppose it's blank in an effort to promote sleep, but right now it's making me restless.

There's nothing to look at except the rolling waves and my brain is full of what ifs. What if the kids need to reach me and they can't? What if Margot forgets that Ollie doesn't eat fish other than fish fingers and that horrible Sara is bullying Millie again at school? What if Amity digs around in my brain and discovers all of the detritus I've tried to keep hidden for years?

It's a relief when there's a gentle knock on the door. I rush to open it. Amity is back.

'I'll show you around and then it's time for lunch,' she says with a warm smile.

I glance at my watch and see that it's already 12:30 pm, grateful that at least I'm allowed to wear the little, silver Longines watch that Haydn gave me as a wedding present. Amity leads me on a quick tour of some more communal rooms, including a meditation room where teepee-like hammocks are strung from the ceiling and big cream-coloured beanbags are scattered across the pale wooden floor. Downstairs there are several treatment rooms with

massage tables, a room with a white space-age looking floatation tank, a large sauna and changing rooms. Then she leads
me to the end of the corridor and slides back a large glazed
door, exposing the exterior where sunloungers are positioned
around the infinity pool. I shiver as it's colder outside than it
looks.

'We keep the pool at a constant thirty-two degrees Celsius
so you can take a dip whatever the weather, and of course if
you'd like a swim in the sea, there's a gate at the bottom of the
garden with access to the beach. We keep it locked for security reasons, but if you need to go out, just ask me or one of
my staff.'

The high fence encircling the property is taller and more
visible on the ground level where the swimming pool is than
it is from my room. Though it's not visible at all from the
main living spaces. This building and outside space has been
cleverly designed.

'So to lunch.' Amity smiles at me. 'We'll be spending
quite a bit of time in my treatment room, because much of
the sleep programme is built around therapy. You'll see that
later, but for now our chef has prepared something delicious
for you.' She leads me to the dining room where there are
women seated at each of the five tables, mostly two to a table.
I glance at them, but no one looks up at me. They're a variety
of ages from twenties to sixties and all of them are concentrating on their food. I wonder if this is one of those places
where you have to chew every mouthful forty times, or something ridiculous. I'm certainly not going to be doing that.
Amity pulls out the chair at the table with one woman and
indicates for me to sit down.

'Enjoy your lunch, ladies,' she says, before retreating.

Well this is awkward. I didn't think I'd be sharing my
meals with strangers.

'Hello, I'm Flo,' the young woman says, extending her

hand. Her blonde hair is tied back with a bobble and her face is reddish with a shine. It looks like she's had an invigorating exfoliation.

'Daisy,' I say.

'I was feeling like I was being given the cold shoulder, having to sit here all alone.' Flo laughs.

A waitress – another young woman wearing a white shirt and blue trousers but with a white apron around her midriff – arrives with a beautifully presented salad and places it in front of me. She fills up my glass with water from a carafe.

'How long have you been here?' I ask Flo, tucking into my salad. It may look pretty but it's unsubstantial, consisting of a variety of salad leaves, a few chopped mini tomatoes and cucumber, bedecked with a couple of nasturtium flowers and a scattering of seeds.

'Three days. It's a pre-wedding stay, a present from my mum.'

'Lucky you,' I say, hoping she doesn't ask me too many questions because I'm certainly not going to tell anyone that I'm a journalist.

I finish the salad quickly and I'm still hungry. I wave to the waitress who hurries over.

'Any chance of having a bread roll?' I ask.

The young girl looks horrified, as if I asked for an illegal drug or something. Flo sniggers.

'I'm sorry,' the waitress mutters and hurries away.

'What have I done?' I ask.

'The cardinal sin,' Flo whispers. I see her looking at someone over my shoulder before she carries on taking slow mouthfuls of her consommé, her eyes now fixed on her soup bowl.

Amity appears next to me and sinks to her knees, talking in a low whisper. 'I know you're here for the sleep programme, but we put all our guests on a restrictive diet before we've fully assessed them. My colleague will take your bloods after lunch and then we'll draw up a bespoke menu for you.'

'I don't need to have my blood taken,' I say. This is not what I expected.

'We're a wellness spa, Daisy. We look at our guests holistically so it's very important to measure how you are when you arrive and then we study the metrics at the end of your stay, so we can see how your health has improved. Additionally, and even more importantly in your case, we need to explore whether you have any underlying medical conditions that might be the root cause of your insomnia. Have you been assessed for sleep apnoea, diabetes or heart disease?'

I shake my head.

I suppose what she's saying makes sense, but I don't like unnecessary prodding by doctors or having my blood taken. I guess I'll just have to swallow this one and hope my stomach doesn't growl too loudly with hunger. If I'd known this was the policy here, I'd have stashed my suitcase full of chocolate biscuits and crisps.

Of course I only have myself to blame. If I'd done my research before coming to The Serenity Spa, I would no doubt have realised that this isn't one of those lovely relaxation places where you have an aromatherapy massage in the morning, a gentle swim in the afternoon followed by half a bottle of fine wine in the evening. Instead, I blocked the whole trip from my mind, shrouded by my exhaustion, as I barely managed to drag myself through each day. I guess this place is like that Austrian spa that one of my followers commented about on my Facebook group.

Thanks, Garth, I think to myself. Amity leaves us with a tight smile.

'Welcome to The Serenity–' Flo grins, '–where your

stomach will growl and your body will relax. Which programme are you on?'

'Insomnia,' I say.

'Oh, I didn't know they did a sleep programme. I'm on the quick weight loss week, because if I don't lose at least half a stone, I'm not going to fit into my wedding dress. To be honest, I'm having a great time here. It's really relaxing and lovely here other than I'm hungry all the time.'

'And *are* you losing weight?' I ask. Flo looks perfectly healthy to me and certainly not overweight, although as we're all dressed in thick white gowns, I suppose we all look the same.

'I'll know when I hop on the scales before I leave.'

We chat for a few more minutes and finish off our minimal lunches with herbal teas, and then another young woman appears at our table, this time dressed in a beauty uniform of a navy tunic and straight legged trousers.

'Daisy, I'm Shayla, Dr Dhingra's assistant. He's ready to see you now.'

'Good luck,' Flo says, as I stand up, wondering if I'm about to be released into the lion's den. I follow her downstairs and into a corner room that Amity didn't show me earlier. A short, wiry man jumps to his feet and pumps my hand up and down.

'Welcome, Daisy. I'm Doctor Samesh Dhingra and I will be doing your full medical checkup.'

The name rings a bell but I can't place him. Perhaps he's one of those celebrity doctors who has treatment rooms on London's Harley Street and is written up in glossy magazines. Perhaps we even wrote a piece on him. It's so frustrating that I can't return to my room and look him up. It makes me realise how utterly wedded I am to my mobile phone.

For the next thirty minutes, Dr Dhingra takes vials of blood, he tests my blood pressure and pulse, listens to my chest, looks in my eyes and ears and weighs me. He asks numerous questions about my health and the health of my parents. I know Amity explained that they do this to work out a bespoke programme of healing for their clients, and as a way of evaluating how well their programme has worked, but it's like having a complete medical for a life policy.

'Is there anything amiss–?' I say.

'I will have all the results for you in a couple of days, and some of the information will be fed back to Amity later today. We like to work quickly. Rest assured, if there's anything wrong with you, we will find it. My initial conclusion is that you are in good health but the lack of sleep is affecting some of your vitals. Amity will explain more.'

I walk out of Dr Dhingra's room feeling positive. My GP would never have given me a complete checkup like the one I just had and I certainly can't afford to go private. Perhaps I really will have a transformation in my sleep by the end of the week.

I wander slowly back to my room, enjoying the total silence in this building and realising how rarely I experience total tranquillity. I smile at the word *Repose* on my door and use the key card in my pocket to let myself in. Inside my room, I walk to the window and open it a few inches, letting the cool sea breeze into the room. Then I lie down on the sumptuous, soft bed and before long I drift off to sleep to the sound of the rolling waves.

4

DAISY

I wake up about an hour later to the sound of gentle knocking on the door.

'Just a moment,' I say, sitting up in bed and rubbing my eyes, shocked that I actually slept.

It's chilly in the room now so I close the window before walking barefoot to the door, pulling the dressing gown belt tighter around my midriff.

'Sorry to disturb you, but Amity would like to see you now.' It's Jenny, the young woman from reception.

I ask her to wait for a couple of minutes while I freshen up and then follow her downstairs to the opposite end of the corridor where I saw Dr Dhingra. She knocks on a door and holds it open for me.

Amity is sitting on a swivel chair in front of a sleek, pale wooden desk that has the look of a high-end designer piece of furniture. She has a notebook balanced on her knee and is holding a pencil. The room has whitewashed walls and several, large house plants dotted around in terracotta containers. There's a scent diffuser machine on the edge of her desk that is releasing a little plume of air scented with lavender and something else I can't determine.

'Come in, Daisy. How are you feeling?' Amity flicks her hair back over her shoulders.

'Surprisingly rested. I drifted off to sleep just now and I never sleep in the afternoons.'

She gestures for me to sit down on a plump armchair covered with a cream fabric, similar to the furniture elsewhere. I notice there's a daybed wedged up against the wall and a voile blind is blocking out the view to the sea through the window to our left. There's a jug of water, an empty glass and a box of tissues placed on a small, glass coffee table that sits between us.

'We're going to start our session today with me telling you a bit about myself, to reassure you that you're in safe hands, and then we'll discuss the basics of the sleep programme. Is that alright with you, Daisy?' Amity tilts her head to one side and her dark shiny hair glints.

'Sure,' I say, settling into the comfortable armchair.

'Being a journalist, I've no doubt that you've done lots of research into me.' Amity smiles.

Actually, I've been totally negligent and have done no research whatsoever but I try not to let that show on my face. 'Please tell me about yourself anyway.' I hope she'll just think I am being polite.

'Okay, a little background on me. I trained as a psychologist many years ago and have been in private practice ever since. I've completed lots of additional training and work closely with colleagues including my mentor, who assesses me regularly to make sure that I am up to scratch.' She winks at me. 'I primarily work with techniques including CBT, which is cognitive behavioural therapy, and aversion therapy otherwise known as desensitisation, and hypnosis. More recently I've taken special interest in helping my clients overcome sleep issues. Have you got any initial questions for me?'

I'm sure I should have but just the sound of her low, gentle voice is making me sleepy. I shake my head.

'In order to break a habit such as insomnia – which incidentally is a word that I don't like to use – we need to understand what triggered the sleeplessness in the first place. Only then can we take steps to change your thought patterns and routines. I need to be clear with you, Daisy, this process can become uncomfortable and sometimes things get worse before they get better. This is totally normal and that's why this programme is so unique, as we are able to give you twenty-four hour support, making sure you feel safe and secure in the knowledge that everything we do is designed to make you better.'

I shift in the comfortable armchair because now I feel nervous. The effects of not being able to sleep are monumental and the thought that things might have to get worse before they get better is something I simply can't grapple with. But it's her words, *we need to understand what triggered the sleeplessness in the first place*, that resound in my head. Could it be that my greatest fear about this process might be exposed? Is she really expecting me to share what triggered the sleeplessness? Frankly, I feel like running out of this place right now. If it wasn't for the fact that Garth sent me here and Hayden and the kids need my income, I might well forego all this luxury and bolt. Amity can try as hard as she likes but I am never going to share what really happened to me with her.

'You look uncomfortable,' Amity says, leaning towards me and placing her hands on her knees.

'No, no, it's fine,' I lie. 'It's just... I've never experienced therapy before and I suppose I was a bit naive coming into this process.'

'Don't you worry. There'll be plenty of lovely relaxing massages and treatments that will make you feel glorious but are designed to treat the symptoms. What I want to do is root out the cause. Does that make sense?'

I nod reluctantly.

'Please trust me, Daisy. If I can cure you of your sleepless-ness–' She glances at the form that I filled in this morning. 'If I can help you increase the number of hours you sleep from an average of two or three – which is shocking by the way, and frankly I don't know how you look so well on so little sleep – to seven or eight hours of deep, relaxing sleep, that will be – excuse the pun – a dream come true for both of us. I will have healed you and you will write a lovely article about the programme, which will help me get more clients.'

I'm relieved that Amity is being upfront about this. She's right: that is the real reason she invited me. I let my shoulders slump and lean back into the chair.

'Tell me about yourself, Daisy. Who are the important people in your life?'

Now we're on comfortable ground. 'I have a wonderful husband called Haydn and we've been together for twelve years. We've got two children, Millie who is eight and Ollie who is six. Home life is good. My husband recently started a new construction business, so I took on more of the load for everything during the past year.'

'Did that coincide with your sleep issues?'

'No. Sleep has been a problem for years.'

'And your work?'

'Honestly, it's pretty easy. I can do it with my eyes closed after all this time but the lack of sleep is affecting my work. I've been finding it hard to concentrate, I've been forgetting things.'

'That's totally normal,' she says, reassuringly. 'So when did sleep become a problem?'

'After the children were born,' I say, trying very hard to maintain eye contact with Amity. If she's as astute a psychologist as she makes out, I assume she'll see straight through my bluffing. I lean in and pour some water into a glass. A slice of lemon from the jug plops in with it and splatters drops of water on the table.

I start to wipe it up with a tissue.

'It's fine, just leave it,' Amity says. 'Are you a perfectionist?'

'Um, sometimes. I used to be I suppose, but now I let things slip. I don't want to but I can't help it.'

'That must be very hard for you,' she says. I nod. 'And what's it like when you go to bed?'

'I try to relax. I do all the things you're meant to. Not looking at my phone or laptop for an hour before bedtime, making sure the room is dark and quiet, which generally it is except when Haydn snores. Having a relaxing bath before bed. But then I lie there for hour after hour and if I do drop off, I wake up with a start after about sixty minutes. And so it goes on.'

'That's a very typical pattern. Tell me what you're thinking about when you're lying awake.'

'That varies from the minutiae of our daily life, worrying about the kids, Haydn's business, what I've forgotten to do at work, to counting sheep, putting in earphones and listening to meditation, trying to imagine I'm on a lovely beach somewhere. Unfortunately nothing works.'

'And quite naturally that's what you've come to expect. The more we think about sleep and worry about not having any, the more likely it's going to evade us.'

I nod, because I know all of this. It's the sort of thing I talk about on my blog.

Amity continues. 'One of the main principles of CBT is based on the fact that we hang on to false beliefs and expectations about the world which can have a negative effect and cause stress and anxiety. So in your case, you have built up a fear around not sleeping. What we need to do is banish that fear so you look forward to bedtime and can fully relax as soon as you get into bed.'

I'm beginning to feel a little bit disappointed because Amity isn't telling me anything I don't already know. Of course I dread going to sleep because I know it's not going to happen. It's not like you can just switch off that thought.

'What I'd like to do is try hypnotherapy on you this week, as I think that could have a dramatic effect. How do you feel about that?'

'Okay.' I've never experienced hypnotherapy but I know it's nothing like stage hypnosis, where suggestible people are made to act like fools. I also know that when you're hypnotised you're still in control, so I'm reasonably confident that I won't accidentally tell Amity any of my darkest secrets.

'Hypnosis works a bit like a mental rehearsal,' she explains. 'We visualise your normal sleep routine and how lying in bed makes your mind race and increases your anxiety. Then we change the scenario, so you can visualise climbing into bed and immediately relaxing into a deep and refreshing sleep. We'll also combine this with positive affirmations and eliminate anything else that might be causing you anxiety around sleep. You'll be in control all of the time.'

'That sounds fine,' I say. I'm surprised at how quickly I go from being disappointed about not learning anything new to being hopeful that Amity might work some magic on me. This week could be amazing, miraculous even, because everything Amity's saying makes sense.

She turns around and reaches for a book, and then swivels back to face me. It is a beautiful leather-covered notebook, with the word *Journal* embossed in gold lettering on the front, which she then holds out to me.

'This is for you. Whenever you return to your room, I

want you to write down your thoughts and hopes and fears in this journal. Keep a track of what's happening both in reality and in your mind. When you wake up, record your dreams.'

I take the heavy notebook from her. It's ironic that even though I'm a writer, I've never been any good at keeping a journal. I tried many a time but gave up after a few days. I often wondered if it was because I'm a writer by day, therefore unwilling to write at night, but the truth is easier. I don't want to write down my innermost thoughts. I'm too worried about Haydn or the kids reading my diary, and if I'm being honest, I can't bear the thought of facing them myself. That's why the Facebook group works so well for me. I can discuss insomnia without delving into my personal issues too deeply.

'Thanks,' I say, balancing the journal on my knees.

'In addition, my team and I will be using relaxation massages, aromatherapy, light therapy, a bespoke diet combined with natural supplements to support your nervous system, and we'll be eliminating any bad sleep habits. We'll be working on every one of your senses. Any questions, Daisy?'

I remember that I'm here not only to enjoy myself and hopefully be cured but also as a journalist. 'What's so different about your programme? I'm aware there are other sleep clinics both in the UK and around the world.'

Amity smiles broadly and leans back in her chair, steepling her fingers. 'To be blunt, it's me. The difference in our programme is the years of experience and research that I've done to develop my techniques. I used to struggle with sleeplessness just like you, Daisy. But I cured myself and that's what I will do for you. Now, why don't we do a short hypnotherapy session, just to ease you into it?'

'Alright,' I say tightly. I was hoping that Amity might give me a more scientific answer but I'm sure there'll be time for that later this week.

'Hop onto the daybed and lie down on your back, making yourself comfortable,' she instructs. She presses a button on a remote control and blackout blinds descend, eliminating all daylight. Amity presses another switch and the walls are lit up with a gentle blue hue. I assume she must have coloured strip LEDs on the floor to create this soothing effect. She places a taupe-coloured, light cotton blanket over me, covering my bare feet and legs, and gives me a silk pillow to put under my head.

'Daisy, I want you to take three deep breaths.' Her voice is low, monotone and soft. 'Breathe in deeply into your abdomen, and slowly out. On the first breath, your eyes will get tired. On the second breath, you will want to close your eyes, and on the third breath, you *will* close your eyes. They will shut tight and your eye muscles won't work. Perhaps you're not sure that this will work. Test it out. Try to open your eyes.'

I flicker my eyes open, somewhat relieved that I still have control of my body.

I sense a smile in Amity's voice as if this was what she expected. 'Now, Daisy, you need to relax the muscles around your eyes some more. You have to *want* it to happen, *expect* it to happen and *watch* it happen. The harder you try to open your eyes, the less your eye muscles will work. Try to open your eyes.'

I do, and to my surprise, my eyes don't open.

'Relax now. When I click my fingers you'll be able to open your eyes easily.' She clicks her fingers and my eyes spring open. 'And when I count to three again, your eyes will close and lock and you won't be able to open them. Want this to happen, expect this to happen and watch this happen. One. Two. Three. Close your eyes and you'll find that they're locked. You're safe, Daisy.'

She then talks me through a relaxation technique I'm

familiar with, tightening and releasing every body part, starting with my toes and ending with the top of my head. And I do feel relaxed, totally at ease, just concentrating on the gentle tone of Amity's voice.

'Now I want you to imagine that you're in your special place. This special place could be a real location, perhaps somewhere you love visiting that makes you feel relaxed and happy, or it could be an imaginary place, for instance a tropical beach or a mountain meadow. Imagine that you're at the top of a beautiful staircase that's going to lead you down to your special place. Feel yourself becoming more relaxed, sleepier, calmer and heavier. Count down from ten to one and as you do, take a step down.'

There's a pause for a moment before she starts speaking again.

'And now we're in your special place. Let the every day world fade away and your mind relax as you go to your special place. Imagine a warm cloud surrounding you. Just drift off and let your mind wander wherever it wants to go. Watch images that come up from your subconscious mind and see them floating and drifting softly and gently up and away. Sink into that wonderful warm, comfortable cloud and know that you are safe, relaxed and happy. Drift and float, feeling sleepier and more relaxed than you've ever felt before. Watch how your thoughts and feelings and memories move around and fade in and out as you listen to my voice. As this wonderful cloud surrounds you, supporting you, everything else becomes more faint – my voice, your thoughts and memories just fading away. Everything becomes more distant and my voice is less clear, further away, and soon you are drifting into a relaxing natural sleep. You will sleep for a while and then, when my voice says your name, you will come out of your sleep. Drift now to sleep. Sleep. Sleep.'

And I do. I really think I sleep, because then I hear

Amity's voice gently saying my name and my eyes flicker open, yet my body feels so heavy, so relaxed.

'Sit up very gently, Daisy,' she says as the blue light fades into a white light.

I swing my legs off the daybed and stretch.

'How are you feeling?'

'Great,' I say, surprising myself, and then I can't stop smiling because if it's really that easy, perhaps Amity *will* cure my insomnia. I'll owe Garth the most enormous thank you.

There's a knock on the door and Jenny comes in with a mug of steaming tea. She hands it to me.

'Thanks, Jenny,' Amity says. 'It's a special herbal tea for you, Daisy, to ground you after the hypnosis. When you've drunk that, I would like us to take a brisk walk on the beach to get some fresh air. That will be the end of your first day, a wonderful one I hope.'

The sun has disappeared and the air has taken on a bitter chill. I suggest to Amity that I nip upstairs to get my coat but she gives me a half smile. 'I want you to go for a short walk just wearing your bathrobe. It's to boost your metabolism.' It seems that she's allowed to wear a woollen coat but I'm not.

I follow her outside and we walk past the swimming pool and take several steps down from the wooden decking. Up close, the wooden fence must be a good seven feet high. She opens a wooden gate set in the fence with a key card and we cross over a patch of grass and then we're on the pebbly beach. The sea looks choppy with white frothy waves. The scent of the salty sea air burns the back of my throat, the cold making me shiver.

'Take your slippers off,' Amity instructs me, raising her voice to be heard over the loud waves. I'm bitterly cold now and the last thing I feel like doing is walking barefoot over these pebbles that are either sharp or slimy, but I do as Amity tells me and pop my slippers into the large pocket of the bathrobe. I follow Amity as she strides quickly down the beach towards the edge of the sea where there's a layer of scum and seaweed. I try not to be a wimp but this is really unpleasant. Amity turns around and smiles at me.

'This is good for you, Daisy. You need to inhale the bracing air and feel the earth through your feet.' It's fine for her to say that wrapped up warmly in her coat and wearing thick-soled white trainers.

We walk briskly, or more like I tiptoe as fast as I can for ten minutes or so, by which time I'm shivering violently and the soles of my city, permanently-shoed feet feel like they've been shredded. At this point I think she takes pity on me, because then she turns around and we walk at a slower pace back to the spa.

'Go and take a hot shower,' Amity suggests, as we stand in the corridor outside my room. 'Please join the others for supper at 6.30 pm. We eat early here to give you time to digest your food before bed. Afterwards, I'd like you to journal how you think your first day went. Sleep well, Daisy.'

And then she walks away and I feel weirdly bereft of her company.

5

AMITY

I t's been a good day. This morning the sun was shining and I woke up in a great mood. I have the house to myself at the moment, and when I'm alone, I like to rise at dawn to watch the sun burst over the horizon and glitter onto the sea. Although it doesn't exactly do that because our house is south, not east facing.

Nevertheless, dawn is my favourite time of day. My husband, Keith, likes to sleep in the dark and insists on blackout blinds. Fortunately, he hasn't been home for nearly a fortnight – not that I told the staff at the spa that news. My home life is none of their business. With the kids at boarding school it's quiet and I like it that way.

The Serinity Spa has been open for seven months and I'm thrilled with the way it's going. We've been booked up pretty much since week one, and although our guests may not be the A-listers that I insinuate are staying here, we've had enough social media influencers to put us on the map. That's the beauty of having a no-phone, no-photo, and a first-name-only policy. It means no one except our staff knows the true identities of our guests, past and present.

I spent such a long time planning the spa, researching other venues all over the globe, thanks to Keith's generosity, and by the time we started planning this place, I knew exactly what I wanted. Recruiting first-class staff has been more of a challenge but money talks and fortunately I have enough of that.

First thing I did this morning after eating a bowl of granola prepared by our wonderful chef at the spa was I jogged along the beach. It's perfect living just five doors down from the spa, although five doors accounts for about half a mile. We're on the smart end of the beach where the properties are spread far apart and privacy can be maintained. After, I used my key card to let myself in through the gate and sauntered along the silent therapy corridor to my personal suite, happy that I saw no one. My personal suite includes a bedroom, should I need to work late or take a mid-afternoon nap, a zen area where I do my yoga and meditations, and a beautiful steam shower room in marble with a shower head that has a myriad of different pressures and lighting effects. I'm going to ask Keith if we can install the same version at home, even though it costs nearly ten grand. I took a quick shower and selected a linen dress from my wardrobe. I keep a selection of work clothes here, all ethically sourced linen combinations.

'Good morning!' I said cheerfully as I walked into the dining room. The staff were busying around as they have been trained to do and I was pleased that everything seemed to be in order. The phone rang as I strode towards the reception desk. Whether Jenny had intended to answer it on the second ring, or whether she was spurred on to do so when she saw me, I wasn't sure. Either way, she answered it exactly as she's been trained to do.

'Gosh, I'd need to check,' Jenny said, glancing at me with a slight look of concern. 'I believe we're fully booked and rarely take such last-minute bookings.' There was a long pause and then Jenny said, 'If you wouldn't mind holding on for a moment, I'll have a discussion with my manager.'

Jenny pressed the mute button and I looked at her with an eyebrow raised. 'It's a woman who wants to make a last-minute booking. She wants to come today, to stay this week. The only room we've got left is Respite.'

Respite is the room that we reserve for emergencies, a small ensuite with views to the rear of the building, unlike our other guest suites that face the sea. I didn't want the room at all, but the architect persuaded me that it would be otherwise unused space and that as we grew, we would need to increase the number of guest rooms.

'Let me talk to her,' I said, holding out my hand for the telephone.

'Good morning, Amity Augustiago speaking.'

'Oh, Amity. What a privilege to speak to you,' the woman gushed. 'My name is Rosemary Burgh and I was hoping that it might be possible for me to come last minute, ideally for your insomnia programme.'

I cringed at the woman's voice and obvious desperation. 'I'm sorry but we're fully booked.'

'I don't need anything fancy,' Rosemary said. 'And I'm in such desperate need of a bit of R & R. Please. I can't tell you how grateful I'd be.'

'I can't get you on the insomnia programme as it's fully booked,' I said. 'However, I have a small room you can stay in and if we can squeeze you in for some treatments, then we'll do our best to do so. No promises though.'

I quoted her the full amount for a premier suite and it was Jenny's turn to raise an eyebrow. 'But I'll need to take payment immediately. I will pass you back to my colleague to organise that.' I handed the phone back to Jenny.

As I walked into the office behind the reception desk, I

couldn't stop the smile from spreading across my face. That woman had just agreed to pay more than enough to cover the cost of the free week we're giving to Daisy McKenzie. I was rather pleased with myself. I sat down in front of the computer and looked through our booked-up calendar.

Our current cohort of guests were making good progress but there was only one person I was really interested in, and that's Daisy.

Now, I reflect back on Daisy McKenzie's first twenty-four hours here. I had everything planned out in great detail and it went perfectly. Daisy is reacting exactly the way I envisaged.

I'm tired after Daisy's hypnotherapy session but I'm still not ready to return to my empty house. Instead, I spend half an hour in my suite doing some restorative yoga and when I'm feeling calm and collected, I walk slowly to the dining room. I stand for a few moments in the shadows watching my guests chomping on their food. Most of them are fundamentally lazy, so it's hardly surprising that they're overweight, unhealthy and miserable. Even if they lose a couple of pounds while they're here, despite all of my team's hard work in re-education, I know that their bad habits will return the moment they're back home.

Not that I care. Of course I'd never ever express my true feelings. I'll just smile sweetly and throw them some encouraging platitudes.

'It's Amity, isn't it?'

I don't recognise the woman so assume she's the idiot who agreed to pay full price for the small room at the back.

'Rosemary?' I ask, smiling as I hold out my hand. She's wearing elasticated grey trousers and a cheap-looking sweatshirt, with hair that is screaming out for a cut and a colour.

This is not the look I expect from my guests so the sooner she's out of those garments the better.

She flushes. 'Yes. It's truly lovely to be here. I've just signed all the papers.' I beckon to Jenny, who is placing papers inside a lever-arch binder, and she hurries over.

'Can you take Rosemary to her room straight away so she can change and be back in the dining room before the kitchen closes?'

'Of course,' Jenny says, but not before I notice a slight frown, because Jenny knows perfectly well that chef will stay here as long as needed and there really is no particular urgency.

When they disappear down the corridor, I return to my position in the shadows to watch the guests.

Daisy walks into the dining room without seeing me. I suppress a shiver. Is this really going to work? I have every reason to believe it will. Daisy McKenzie may be here to cure her insomnia, but I have other plans, plans that are going to make her insomnia feel like a little scrape. Daisy needs to know what true pain feels like. She is going to suffer.

6

DAISY

After lathering up with some wonderfully scented body wash in a hot shower, as well as checking the soles of my feet, which surprisingly are only dirty and not lacerated, I put on the fresh towelling robe and slippers that have been lain out for me on my bed, and make my way to the dining room. Although I didn't enjoy the short but brisk walk on the beach, I have to admit that I feel lighter somehow, refreshed even. I sit down at the table with my dinner companion, Flo.

'How was your afternoon?' she asks, leaning back in her chair languidly and stifling a yawn.

'Not as relaxing as yours, I suspect,' I say with a grin.

'Yeah. I had a session in the floatation tank and then a hot-stone massage. It was wonderful.'

'Lucky you.'

The waitress arrives with our food and to my delight, I see from the cutlery that I am being given a three course meal. For starters, I have a small but very tasty fishcake with salad. My main is a chicken fillet with roasted sweet potatoes and spinach – a hearty meal in comparison to lunchtime's offering. I'm even offered a dessert – a choice of sorbet or dark chocolate and orange mousse. I choose the latter.

Unfortunately Flo isn't so lucky. Her starter is a green juice, her main course is salad with a thin slice of mackerel and her dessert is a simple, berry fruit salad. She stares at my food with greedy eyes and I am filled with guilt. Surely it's unfair to put Flo, who is on a weight loss programme, on the same table as me? I eat hurriedly and refrain from commenting on how delicious the food is.

Flo tells me all about her fiancé and the church wedding they're having in six weeks time. It will be followed by a reception in a gigantic teepee in a Hampshire field. I think back to Haydn and my wedding. To Margot's eternal disappointment, we opted for a low-key ceremony. Even if I'd dreamed of the full white fairy-tale event (which I hadn't), I wasn't in the right place emotionally to throw a great big party. I told Haydn that it would be more prudent to save the money for a downpayment on our house and he agreed. We got married at Horsham registry office followed by drinks for twenty in a local pub, where Dad proceeded to get drunk. Margot wore a hat nevertheless.

A tall woman with fine, frizzy-grey hair approaches our table. Her skin is smooth so it makes it difficult to assess her age.

'Are you enjoying it here, ladies?' Her voice has the slight twinge of an accent, Dutch perhaps?

Flo and I glance at each other. 'Yes,' Flo says.

'I just arrived and I'm so excited!' She bounces from foot to foot, her smile showing off teeth that could do with a dentist's attention. She then lowers her voice. 'Is one of you Daisy?'

'Yes, that's me,' I say, wondering why she's asking.

She claps her hands together and emits a little squeal. 'Oh goodness, I can't believe I'm actually getting to meet you!'

Jenny appears and places a hand on the woman's arm. 'Your table is ready. Please can you follow me.'

Reluctantly, the woman turns away from us and follows Jenny across the room.

'Are you famous?' Flo asks.

I laugh. 'No. She must have me mixed up with someone else.'

'But she called you Daisy.'

'It's strange,' I admit.

Whenever I look up, I catch the tall woman staring at me. Then she breaks into a broad grin and wriggles her fingers at me whenever our eyes lock. It's awkward and I'm eager to get out of the dining room.

After supper, Flo leads me into the living room where the ladies who left the dining room before us are sipping herbal teas and chatting quietly. Flo and I sit on a sofa next to a coffee table with an array of board games and jigsaw puzzles. A couple of women are playing chess but everyone else is chatting.

A waitress comes in and gives Flo and me herbal teas, not that either of us ordered them. And then the frizzy-haired woman enters the living room and makes a beeline for me. There isn't a chair next to us so she perches on the arm of the sofa, leaning in much too close, her garlic breath unpleasant, invading my personal space. I can see Flo is trying hard not to giggle as I shift my body away from the woman.

'Daisy, it's such a blessing to be here with you.'

'Do I know you?' I ask, hoping that she's not someone important who I met recently and I'm not putting my foot in it.

'Only by name. We've never met in person which is why I'm so excited to meet you in the flesh. I'm Rosemary Burgh.' She places a hand on my shoulder and gazes at me expectantly. The name means absolutely nothing and I look at her blankly. For a split second her face falls.

'Well, I can't expect you to know us all. I'm one of your most ardent followers on *Can't Sleep And Going Crazy*. I was the ninety-eighth person to join your group.'

'So you *are* famous!' Flo interrupts.

I laugh. This is awkward. 'Not at all. I had a blog and now have a Facebook group for people who have sleep problems.'

'She's our lovely guru,' Rosemary says. 'What she writes is so wise and inspiring and I can't begin to tell you how amazing it is to meet you in person. When I get my phone back there are going to be hundreds of thousands of people who will be so jealous.'

Flo's eyes widen. 'You've got hundreds of thousands of followers?'

'They're not following me.' I wish I could get back to my room right now. 'It's just a popular group for fellow insomniacs.'

'She's too modest, too lovely,' Rosemary says, stroking my forearm. I jerk my arm away and Flo tries but fails to control a snigger.

'How did you know who I am?' I remember Amity explicitly saying that she keeps guests' identities secret and that only first names are used here.

'You told the group you were coming here!' she exclaims, her eyes wide and her forehead creasing.

Did I? Perhaps I did, I simply don't recall. I don't have access to the internet so I can't check.

'Are you also doing the sleep programme?' Flo asks.

'Alas no. They were fully booked up for that. I'm here for the Banish Stress programme. What about you?'

'Weight loss,' Flo says.

'You don't look like you need that!' Rosemary exclaims.

Everything is a little too exuberant with her, as if she speaks with several exclamation marks after her sentences.

'I'm getting married and need to fit into the dress,' Flo explains.

'That's lovely,' Rosemary says. 'I love a wedding.' It sounds like she's angling for an invitation.

I glance at my watch and see it's already 9 pm, and I realise with a pang that I've missed the children's bedtime for the first time ever. By now, they will both be tucked up in bed. If I was home I'd have read them stories and showered them with kisses whether they wanted it or not. Haydn and I might be chatting over a bottle of shared wine or watching some television in silent companionship. I wonder what Margot did with the children, whether they were well behaved.

I have to control myself and not start crying; I'm missing them so much. I know it's the exhaustion that's making me overemotional but it's hard leaving Millie and Ollie behind.

'If you'll excuse me,' I say, standing up. 'I'm really tired.' And I am. It's not the bone-aching weariness that I normally experience but a real, heavy tiredness, as if I might actually sleep.

'Me too,' Rosemary says, doing an exaggerated yawn that frankly looks fake.

'Sleep well both of you,' I say.

'I'll walk with you.' Rosemary gets up so hastily she bumps her leg on the coffee table; the empty cups jangle in the saucers.

'I need to go to reception,' I say, eager to shrug her off. She looks disappointed but after a moment's hesitation, walks off in the opposite direction towards the bedroom corridor. I pad over to the glass reception desk, but there's no one there, so I ring the little gold bell.

A young man appears. 'How can I help you, ma'am?'

'I was wondering if I could call home. I'd like to say goodnight to my children.' It seems farcical that I'm requesting permission to use my own phone.

'I'm very sorry but unfortunately that's not allowed. We have a strict no contact with the outside world policy as I'm sure Ms Augustiago explained to you. However if you would like me to call on your behalf, then I can send your best wishes and check that everything is alright.'

'I suppose so,' I say, feeling dejected now. 'Please can you let my husband know that I don't have my phone with me and explain your no-phone policy to him, because he'll worry if he can't get a hold of me?'

'Of course,' the young man says.

How am I going to last a whole week without speaking to my family?

I write down our home telephone number and wait for a moment, hoping that he'll call while I'm there, but he throws me a look of pity and disappears into the office, closing the door behind him. I wait for a few minutes but I don't hear anything and he doesn't reappear, so I walk slowly back to my room, that familiar feeling of unease bouncing around my gut.

As I slip under the duvet and relax into the gorgeous, soft and smooth linen, I reach for the journal that Amity gave me and grab the wooden pen from my bedside table. It has thick parchment pages that seem too lovely to spoil. I can't stop thinking about the kids, whether Haydn has locked and bolted the back door, whether they're safe. It's so hard not to imagine the worst; that tonight, the first night I haven't been there in years, *he* will come knocking on the door. Or perhaps some horrendous firework will be shoved through the letter box. Or maybe Margot had an accident on the way home from school and they're all in hospital.

Just as these horrible scenarios are playing out in my

head, Amity's voice fills the room. I jump. The pen falls to the floor and my heart thuds in my chest.

'It's time to go to sleep now, Daisy. The lights are going to go off and I want you to listen to my voice.'

Where the hell is she? I glance around the room, but the curtains are pulled tightly and I was just in the bathroom so I know she's not there.

'Relax, Daisy. It's time to go to sleep.'

'Amity, what's going on?' I ask, my voice hoarse and high-pitched. But I get no answer.

It eventually dawns on me that they must have a one-way speaker system in the room so that I can listen to her voice but she can't hear me. But where are the speakers? I glance around the room, at the ceiling, the walls, but there are no grills or obvious signs of an in-built speaker system.

And then the lights go out and the room is plunged into inky blackness. There isn't a chink of light coming from anywhere, not from under the room's door – as there often is in hotels – through the curtains, or even a glow from a light in the bathroom. I don't even have a bedside clock. So all I can do is shuffle down in bed and listen to Amity's voice as it fills the room.

Once again she talks me through clenching and releasing all the muscles in my body. Then I'm descending the staircase, arriving on a beautiful sandy beach with an azure sea, palm trees swaying and coconuts lying on the water's edge. The sun is beating down on my body making my limbs feel languid.

But despite feeling so relaxed and with Amity's voice curling around me magically, I'm still conscious that I'm in a comfortable bed in her spa and not at home where I should be, keeping my family protected from danger.

'Now you're entering a room where you are perfectly safe. There is nothing for you to do, nothing for you to think about. If you're still awake I want you to move to the side of this imaginary room where you'll find several tins of black paint, lots of brushes and containers full of cleaning fluid to clean the brushes. Take a brush and start painting the wall. As you begin to paint over the light wall, imagine you're painting over all of your unwanted thoughts. Let them go. Paint until the walls and ceiling and door are completely black.'

And then I don't hear any more.

I wake with a start, gasping, adrenaline coursing through my veins, my heart pumping loudly, my breathing shallow.

What was that? What did I hear?

I sit bolt upright in bed, blinking hard to try to recapture the light I'm sure I just saw, my ears straining to pick up the sound that woke me. But I can't see a thing in the darkness and the only sound is my own ragged breathing. I fumble on the bedside table trying to feel for the switch on the bedside lamp. I find it and press it but nothing happens. Has the bulb or fuse gone? I shift across the big bed and feel for the bedside lamp on the other side, but that doesn't work either. What the hell?

I swing my feet out of bed and lower them to the soft carpet. I grip the side of the bed as I walk around it and make my way to the window, one hand stretched out in front of me, the other moving from the bed to the wall. When I feel the curtains I pull them apart.

My eyes adjust slowly to the night sky and the sea outside. It's a cloudy night so I can't see much other than outlines. Leaving the curtains open, I walk carefully into the bathroom and am relieved when a blue light comes on at the skirting board level so I can at least see where the toilet and sink is. I switch the main light on but nothing happens. Have all the fuses gone? If so, why are there low-level blue lights? Could they be on a different circuit?

Afterwards, I return to the bedroom and fumble around to find my watch on the bedside table. I carry it into the bathroom, but it's too dark to tell the time. I can't settle back in bed. My heart is still beating too fast and I feel a deep unease.

How I wish Haydn was here. The bed feels cold without him and although I moan about his sporadic snoring and the way he hogs the duvet, his presence calms me. Even when I'm sleeping in the spare room, I am reassured knowing he is next door. Here I'm all alone and although I can't work out why, I'm scared. I wonder if I should be here. Perhaps I should just go home in the morning, back where I belong. But no, I can't do that. Garth would have every right to accelerate disciplinary action against me and I'd be throwing away an opportunity that most people would give their right hand for. Insomnia is my penance but perhaps I'm not ready to forgive myself yet.

I toss and turn for hours, mentally writing a post for my blog, doing anything I can to distract myself from the fear of what might be happening to Millie and Ollie. What if one of them stops breathing in their sleep? Or what if the house is broken into?

I climb out of bed and shut the curtains, then open them again and welcome the pale morning light when it arrives about 4.30 am. I was so hopeful yesterday evening, but those early thoughts of a cure for my insomnia were clearly wishful thinking.

7

DAISY

I t feels like I only just drifted off to sleep when I'm brutally awoken by Amity's cheerful voice coming through the hidden intercom in the ceiling, or wherever it's concealed.

'Good morning, Daisy. I hope you slept well. It's time to get up now. We have lots of great things for you to do today, especially designed to help improve your sleep tonight. One of my colleagues will collect you to take you to breakfast in half an hour, and I'll see you later.'

I feel absolutely shattered. My head is pounding, my neck and shoulders ache and my legs feel too heavy to work. I force myself out of bed and plod towards the bathroom where I take a long shower that wakes me slightly. As I'm shrugging on the bathrobe, I notice a piece of paper that has been slipped under my door.

Hello, just to let you know that your husband and children are fine and wish you a good night. They send you love.

I wish I'd seen that note last night as I might have slept

better. But what if something really happened to them during the night? How would I know? Just because they were alright at 9 pm doesn't mean something didn't happen subsequently.

At 6.30 am there is a knock on the door and young Jenny is standing in the corridor dressed in a starched white shirt, looking bright and perky.

'Good morning, Daisy. I'm here to take you to breakfast. The chef was wondering how you'd like your eggs.'

'Um, I'm not sure if I want any,' I say.

'Oh, you have to have eggs. They're so nutritious and delicious.'

I control an inappropriate snigger, wondering if she works for the egg marketing board. I thought I was here to relax, not to be told what I have to eat. On the other hand I'm too exhausted to put up a fight.

'I'd like a boiled egg, well done please,' I say.

'Perfect, I'll tell the chef.'

There's only one other guest in the dining room sitting at the table farthest away from mine and I'm relieved it's not Rosemary. She mutters good morning and returns to her omelette. I wonder if Flo and the others on the weight loss programme aren't subject to the same strict sleeping hours as I am. I feel a wave of envy. I'd do anything to go back to bed because right now I reckon I could sleep.

I'm brought a deep-red juice that looks more appetising than yesterday's green juice, and it tastes pretty good too – sweet and refreshing at the same time. I'm eating a bowlful of homemade granola with almond milk when Amity comes bouncing into the room. She's wearing white skinny jeans and a loose, pale-grey shirt that hangs to her thighs. Her hair is tied back in a low ponytail and she looks much too radiant and wide eyed for this time of the day. She makes a beeline for my table and sits down opposite me.

'How was your night, Daisy?'

'I drifted off to sleep during your meditation but then I woke up suddenly in the middle of the night. I've no idea what the time was as I couldn't switch the lights on. I assume the fuses must have gone in my bedroom or something.'

'Oh no–' she laughs, '–we do that on purpose. We make sure that you can't be disturbed with light or noise. It's all about mitigating sensory overload.'

'Isn't that dangerous, against health and safety regulations?'

Amity looks affronted. 'Absolutely not. We're knee deep in risk assessments, and in the unlikely case of an emergency, all the lights will work. Look, I don't want you to worry. It's perfectly normal that you would have had a difficult sleep last night. Frankly, if you hadn't I would have wondered why you're here. Our programme takes time to work and you haven't even been here thirty-six hours yet. We'll do a deeper dive today to find out what is causing your sleeplessness.'

She catches the attention of one of the waitresses and orders a juice called *Feed My Soul*. My egg arrives, along with slithers of finely cut avocado and two slices of seeded bread. Amity indicates that I should eat and then moves her chair closer to mine.

'I don't want to worry you, Daisy, but Doctor Dhingra has emailed me the results of your medical. You do have a few health problems that are definitely caused by your sleeplessness. Unfortunately your heart is similar to a woman twenty years older than you. You've got hypertension and at the moment you're headed for diabetes unless we take proactive steps to halt it. Also your cognitive function is low. All in all, we need to change your way of life and we're going to start that right away, hence the breakfast that Doctor Dhingra has suggested chef makes for you. I'm so glad that you came to The Serenity Spa because if you hadn't, well frankly, you

could be dead of a heart attack in the next five years and that
would be truly terrible.'

I let my knife and fork drop onto my plate with a clatter.
This comes as a bolt from the blue. I haven't been on great
form but I had no idea that my health – no my life, was at
risk. Deep down I know that chronic sleeplessness has a
negative effect but this news is terrifying. I simply can't afford
to get ill. I've got two young children who need me and I'm
the breadwinner. I want to live a long, healthy life, to see my
kids settle down and have children of their own. Isn't that
what all parents dream of?

The shock must show on my face because Amity leans
over and pats my arm.

'I don't want you to worry,' she says. 'We have everything
under control and frankly this is good news. There's nothing
worse than burying your head in the sand until it's too late.
By the time you leave here you will be firmly on track to
turning your health around. My mission is to make a
profound difference to your life, Daisy. That's what this week
is all about.'

I smile weakly. I need to believe Amity's words and she's
given me the push to make an appointment with my GP next
week as soon as I get home. She's probably right that it's a
good thing these health issues are discovered now.

'Right, I need to get going,' Amity says, having downed
her juice. She stands up and curls her fingers around the
back of her chair. 'We'll have our next counselling session at
10 am in my therapy room, and after that, I'll share your
schedule for the day. Please have a swim in the pool, or join
the yoga class my colleague, Fran, is running at 8.30 am. I'll
see you later, Daisy.'

And then she's gone in a perfume of complicated scents,
which I'm sure are different from yesterday.

.   .   .

I DON'T GO for a swim or take the yoga class. Instead I lie on my bed (which was made up while I was at breakfast) and doze, trying to prevent horrific images of me in the back of an ambulance or Haydn standing at my graveside. Yes, I know I'm catastrophising and I know that's largely a result of my lack of sleep, but it's near impossible to cast aside the negative images when you've just been given bad news. Time passes slowly and it's a relief when it's 9:50 am and time to go to Amity's room.

Today her walls are lit up in a pale shade of pink – rather pretty and quite surprising. I wonder what the different colours mean. She beckons for me to sit in the comfy armchair.

'This morning, I want to probe deeper to uncover the true reason why you haven't been sleeping. We're going to start with your childhood.'

I let out a silent sigh of relief. I have no secrets in my youth.

'Tell me about family life when you were young.'

'I had a very ordinary, happy childhood. My parents had a great marriage. My brother and I went to the local primary school, which we used to walk to, and then to a local state school. Mum stayed at home and Dad worked as a telecoms engineer. We used to go on holiday in their caravan and visited all sorts of places, from Scotland to France and Italy. We didn't have loads of money but we had enough. Honestly, there was nothing weird about it.'

'Did you have friends, Daisy?'

'Yes, of course, and it's what happened to my best friend that made me want to become a journalist. She had a very rare bone cancer called Ewing's Sarcoma. Even the doctors didn't know what it was, but there was a journalist at our local paper who wrote a story about Josie and through her article loads of money was raised, and awareness of the disease became wider. Josie was one of the lucky ones and she's still going strong today. I thought it was amazing that you could write stories and change people's opinions, and raise awareness. I turned into an idealist.'

'You must have been very bright and focused to become a journalist.'

'I suppose I was,' I say, looking towards the window wistfully.

'Did you go to university?'

'Yes. My parents were so proud. I studied communications, got a first-class degree, spent six months working on a local paper and then I got my big break. I was accepted onto the training scheme of *The Standard*. It was a dream come true.'

'Tell me about it.'

'In those early days I did all the jobs no one else wanted to do, but I relished it. I was on the news desk, often working crazy hours, but it wasn't all stalking politicians and celebrities. There was a lot of boring stuff. Hanging around court, following up leads on the phone, detailed fact checking... but there was such a buzz working there. We were living on adrenaline, booze and cigarettes; we worked hard and played hard and goodness, we really partied. I fell in love too... well, had an affair with an older journalist.'

I let my gaze soften as I think of Rob. He was twenty years my senior, rugged, knowledgable and I'm not proud of it, but he was married. I knew I was just one of a long line of women he had affairs with but it was exciting while it lasted. Looking back, I realise how selfish I was. I don't think I gave a second thought to his wife.

'You look very wistful, Daisy,' Amity comments.

'Just the good old days of my youth.'

'Are you sure that's all it is? You seem to come to life when you talk about your job as a journalist at *The Standard*. Your whole face lights up. I wonder, has your life to date met your younger self's expectations?'

I wish Amity hadn't asked that question. Now I want to retreat back inside myself, forget about those fun and exciting days.

'Well?' she probes.

'I have a happy family life which is everything I always dreamed of.'

'But on the work front?'

I shrug my shoulders.

'You are more than just your family, Daisy. You need to feel fulfilled in every aspect of your life to be truly content.'

I burst into tears. I know it's stupid, pathetic, selfish, but Amity has hit on a raw nerve. Of course I feel like I've let myself down by working for a silly self-indulgent luxury magazine. This isn't where I imagined myself fifteen years ago, of course not. But things happen. I have a job, I earn a living, my name is featured under the articles I write and things could be so much worse.

She pushes the box of tissues towards me and I take one, rubbing my eyes and blowing my nose.

'These questions are designed to get to the root of your problems, Daisy. It's totally natural that you're upset about life's disappointments. We all are to some degree or another. How long did you stay in your job with *The Standard*?'

I squeeze the tissue into a tight ball and take a deep breath. I don't want to talk about this any more.

'Honestly, in the scheme of my life, it's only a minor thing,' I say, trying but probably failing to smile. 'I think it's the tiredness that sets me off; it makes me oversensitive. You see, my life is really great and that's why the sleep issue doesn't make much sense. My husband is amazing. He works hard, he's kind, he does his fair share around the house, he's faithful and a great dad.'

'Mmm,' Amity says, leaning back in her chair. That one syllable suggests she doesn't believe me and that's riling. Haydn is wonderful. 'But obviously your work situation isn't as fulfilling as you hoped. Do you think perhaps that your lack of fulfillment at work could be contributing to your sleep deficit?'

I shrug my shoulders again.

'Let's explore that, shall we?'

'I'm sorry, Amity, but I don't feel like it. I'm exhausted.' I glance at my watch. 'I know it's only 10:20 am but my head is stuffed full of cotton wool.'

I think I see a flash of annoyance pass over her face but it morphs instantly into a smile. She tilts her head. 'Of course, I totally understand. This process can be very gruelling.' She turns to her desk, picks up a piece of printed paper and hands it to me.

'This is your programme for today. I've included lots of exercise because I want you to be physically exhausted by bedtime. This will have the curious effect of making you physically tired but mentally alert, but by 10 pm, all you'll want to do – and will do – is sleep.'

I look at the timetable and frankly I want to sob. It involves a spinning class, a swim in the pool, hot yoga, a jog on the beach, and the only activity listed that I actually want to do – a massage late afternoon.

As I walk slowly back to my room, my feet as heavy as lead, I feel a surge of annoyance. This isn't school or even a boot camp, this is a spa. And if I don't feel like doing an activity then I damn well won't. My only commitment is to write a review of my experience at The Serinity Spa after I leave, and whether or not I follow the exercise regime won't affect that. What's Amity going to do if I don't follow her rules? Kick me out? Quite frankly that would be a relief.

mity's questions about my past leave me feeling unsettled. I suppose it's the mark of a good psychologist to needle out the portions of one's past that are causing problems in the present, but I didn't come here to feel worse. I don't want to be analysed and assessed, I just want to sleep. Yes, I know there's no gain without pain and all of those clichés, but I simply can't go there. Bring on the aromatherapy massages and reflexology please.

I have no intention of jogging along the beach but I don't mind a gentle walk, although I'm certainly not going to venture out again in that damned bathrobe and slippers. I return to my room, pull on my jeans, trainers, a thick jumper and my anorak, and walk back to reception.

'You're dressed!' Jenny says, a look of surprise on her face, although why I don't know. It's hardly normal to be wandering around in a bathrobe all day, especially in a public place.

'Amity suggested I go for a jog on the beach. I need to be dressed for that.'

'Of course,' she says, yet her face is an expression of doubt. 'Would you like the key card to get in and out of the gate?'

'Yes please.'

Jenny types rapidly on a keyboard and then hands me a key card. 'It's timed so it'll let you out now but you need to return within two hours, otherwise it will stop working. At that point you'll have to walk almost two miles to get back here along the main roads.'

I frown.

'Security,' she says. 'We're on a public beach and we need to make sure our guests are protected.'

It sounds more like we're prisoners than guests but I bite my tongue.

I follow the path that Amity took me on yesterday and feel a sense of relief once I'm outside the perimeter of the spa. It's not like I'm having a bad time there, it's just a little too intense for my liking. I walk east along the beach, in the direction of Worthing, I think. The air is damp and chilly but the sea brings me to life, and I decide that our next family holiday will be by the seaside. Our finances won't stretch to a trip abroad, but Wales would be nice, or Cornwall perhaps. I keep an eye on the time and am back well before my lock-out. After changing back into my bathrobe, Jenny ushers me into the dining room.

To my disappointment Flo isn't there. It's strange how we have absolutely nothing in common but I like the young woman. I'm tucking into a chicken salad with some sweet potato chips and realise it's the first time in well over a decade that I am sitting alone at a table. I used to think being by myself wouldn't bother me but here I have nothing to distract me; no book, no phone, only my unwelcome worries. Perhaps tonight I'll bring the journal and pen with me and write some notes for my review.

And then Rosemary appears, plonking herself down in Flo's chair.

'I hope you don't mind, Daisy, but I had a word with Jenny and asked if I could swap table partners. The woman I'm seated with–' she glances over her shoulder at a peroxide, Botoxed blonde, '–well, she's rather vacuous and we have nothing in common. I'm not even sure if she knows what the word insomnia means!' Rosemary laughs loudly. 'Anyway, the answer was yes, so long as Flo isn't here, which is marvellous. I've been desperate to have a one-on-one.'

My heart sinks.

'Now tell me, what's the programme like? Is Amity as fabulous as she seems?'

'It's... well, it's early days. But so far so good.' For some reason I feel disinclined to open up to Rosemary, perhaps because I want to formulate my own views and share my experiences in my article. I wonder if Rosemary knows I'm a journalist. I've never shared that information on my blog or Facebook group.

'If it works for you then it's going to work for the rest of us too and that's so exciting.'

It dawns on me then that perhaps it's no coincidence that Rosemary is here now, that she booked herself in The Serinity Spa because she knew I was coming. The thought appals me, yet I can't bring myself to ask her the question directly.

'I dipped into my life savings to come here,' Rosemary says. 'But it's worth every penny, isn't it? It's lovely.'

I smile tightly, feeling rather guilty it's costing me nothing.

'You're married with children, aren't you?' she says. 'And you work for that fancy magazine.'

This is getting worse; the woman has researched me,

although I suppose it wouldn't be that difficult if you set your mind to it.

'Horsham's such a lovely market town but it's a hike for you to have to get up to London every day. I don't know how you do it. How old are your little ones?'

'Eight and six,' I say wondering how the hell she knows where I live and work.

'Lovely ages.'

I need to direct the conversation away from me. 'Do you have children?'

'Oh no. I was never lucky enough but I have lots of little friends and they keep me busy.'

'Little friends?'

'I have seven cats. They're my life and I can't tell you how stressful it was convincing my neighbours to pop in and feed my lovelies. I created a rota and I just pray it all goes well. I have security cameras at home so I can see them when I'm at work. The thought of not being able to check in with them... To be honest, Daisy, I nearly walked straight back out of here when Amity told me about the no-phone rule, but then I thought if Daisy McKenzie can do it, then so can I.'

I cough to dislodge a rocket leaf that has caught the back of my throat. This woman is freaking me out and her overuse of the word lovely is grating. I have no idea why she holds me in such high esteem. I haven't even written a book, I just write little snippets on my blog and manage the Facebook group. That doesn't make me special.

'What's your programme for this afternoon?' Rosemary asks, taking a large mouthful of chicken.

'I'm not sure.' I can just imagine that if I say I'm going swimming or doing hot yoga then she'll follow suit.

As soon as I'm done with a delicious fruit tart, I push back my chair, not waiting for Rosemary to finish.

'Sorry to be rude,' I say, 'but I need to take a nap.' Rosemary does look affronted but I'll deal with her later; she really isn't my problem. I hurry back to my room, collapse on my bed and to my surprise, I doze off for a couple of hours.

'DAISY, it's Jenny speaking. You have your massage in ten minutes. Please come to reception and I'll take you to your treatment room.' The disembodied voice still startles me but at least it's not the shock it was last night.

After splashing my face with water, I hurry along the corridor to the main hallway where Jenny jumps up from her desk and walks towards me with a smile.

'How does your voice get into my room?' I ask.

She laughs. 'We have an intercom system, a bit like they have on cruise liners where the captain can talk to everyone in case of an emergency.'

'Oh,' I say, because I've never been on a cruise.

'It's a one-way system so you can hear us but we can't hear you.'

In the treatment corridor, she knocks on a door and then opens it to reveal a small, dark room with a massage bed in the centre covered in fluffy white towels. A short, bearded man dressed in a navy T-shirt and navy trousers stands to one side.

'This is Quinn, your massage therapist,' Jenny says. Quinn nods his head deferentially and I try not to show my surprise that my massage therapist is a man. I'm not prudish, it's just that no one has seen me naked except for doctors and Haydn, and well, I wasn't expecting this. I'm lying to myself, perhaps I am prudish.

'Enjoy,' Jenny says as she slips away.

'I'll leave the room whilst you undress,' Quinn says in heavily-accented English.

Hurriedly, I shed my robe and bra and slip underneath

the heated towels, lying on my stomach. A couple of minutes later he returns. He pours some warm oil onto my back and then starts the massage. But this is no gentle affair, he is digging his fingers into my spine, roiling the muscles, placing all his weight into my shoulders. This hurts. No, it really hurts.

I let out a yelp.

'It's painful?' he asks.

'Yes, very.'

But he doesn't reduce the pressure, in fact I think he's putting even more weight into my sore back and I'm not sure that I can take this.

'I'm sorry, but it really hurts. Can you be more gentle please?'

'Yes, but it won't be effective. You want results, no?'

He does reduce the pressure but it's still sore and frankly, this isn't at all what I was hoping for or expecting. There's no gentle music, just Quinn's rather laboured breath and the squelching sound of his fingers digging into me. Rather than relaxing me, it's making me upset and silly as it is, tears spring to my eyes and leak into the paper mat on which I'm lying.

'This is part of process. We need to put pressure on muscles to get them to release,' Quinn says in broken English. 'Amity says good for you, but I be more gentle now.'

'Thank you,' I murmur.

By the time he finishes, I feel bruised and battered; muscles I didn't know I had are screaming out. I drag myself back to my room and pour a hot bath, tipping in several capfuls of a wonderfully scented bath oil. Half an hour later I feel considerably better, although totally exhausted. I feel a bit stupid now, perhaps I was being pathetic.

. . .

I WAKE UP WITH A START. There's loud music playing in my room. Actually in my room! It's some sort of dance music with a heavy beat and it's deeply shocking. It's still light outside but all I want to do is drop back into sleep. If only this damned music would stop. I groan and heave myself up in bed. And then the music fades and Amity's voice comes through.

'Daisy, it's time for supper. You need to hurry, otherwise there won't be any food left.'

What the hell? My brain feels soggy, as if it can't process properly, although surprisingly, a lot of the aches in my body have gone. It's only my shoulders that feel sore. As I rub my eyes and glance at my watch, two things hit me. Firstly, I've slept for two hours, and secondly, is there a hidden camera in this room? If so, that's a horrific thought.

But surely not, that would be illegal. Amity's hardly going to do something like that when she's entertaining me, a journalist. I can just imagine the sensational headlines.

After splashing water on my face and running a comb through my hair, I make my way along the corridor to the dining room. All the other guests are well into their meals but I'm glad to see Flo has returned to our table and that Rosemary is seated on the opposite side of the room.

Flo lifts her eyes and nods at me as she carries on chewing.

'Have you got hidden speakers in your room?' I ask as I sit down.

'Yup. Freaked me out the first time music came on.'

I let out a silent sigh of relief; so it's not only me. The waitress hurries over with a substantial piece of quiche and another salad.

'I hope it's still warm,' she says. I thank her.

Flo seems more subdued than usual. 'Are you alright?'

When she looks up at me there are tears welling in her big blue eyes.

'Not really. Our flat was broken into last night and it was horrible. Thank goodness we don't have children because the burglars had a knife with them and my fiancé got hurt.'

'Oh no! That's terrible. Is he alright?'

'He says he is. He got a couple of stitches to his hand in the hospital. All Si said is he was so glad I wasn't there. But if I'd been there I would have screamed and they might have run away.'

'That's awful, Flo. Don't you want to leave and go home to him?'

'Yeah, of course, but Si said I'm safer staying here. The police said that sometimes they come back for more – not that we've got fancy things, just a big telly and electronics and stuff. I don't care about the things, I just want him to be safe. I told him to go stay with his parents but I don't know if he will.'

I lean across the table and pat Flo's hand. 'What a terrifying thing to happen.'

It gets me thinking and not in a good way. What if we're burgled too? It happened before, two years ago. It was the summer holidays and the kids were both on a sleepover. I got home from work to find the back door slightly ajar. Someone had busted the lock and splintered the door frame. I was terrified. I tiptoed through the house with my phone in my hand while on a call to the police. The living room had been tipped upside down as had our bedroom, but everything else was untouched. I couldn't find a single thing missing. My jewellery was still there, as were our passports, computers and cameras. It didn't make any sense, except to me it did.

The police said it was a random attack and we were lucky; the burglars must have been disturbed which was why they didn't take anything. But it wasn't a random attack. It was a warning. I knew exactly who had done it, except I couldn't prove a thing so I had to keep quiet. The police didn't even bother dusting for fingerprints but if they had, I know what they would have found. The warnings come on average once a year. They're different each time and always horrible.

Flo and I don't talk much after that and I'm glad, because fear is curdling in my stomach, not for myself but for my family. I'm going to have to call them. It's ridiculous that I can't speak to my own children. I'm no longer hungry and when Flo leaves the table, so do I.

Jenny is on reception. 'I know I'm not meant to call my husband and children but I really need to know that they're okay,' I say, drumming my fingers on her glass desk. She looks at me, her forehead wrinkled with concern, and I suspect a little pity too.

'But Amity–'

'I know what the rules are but I'm a guest here not a prisoner. You can either give me my mobile back or perhaps I can use your landline.'

'I'm not sure–'

'Can I speak to Amity?'

'She's left for the evening.'

Jenny is clearly out of her depth here and it really isn't her fault, so I soften my voice. 'Look, why don't I use your landline and you can listen to the conversation. All I want to do is say goodnight to my children. That's not breaking any law, is it?'

Jenny pales but she stands up and hands me the phone receiver.

'Thank you,' I say as I dial our home number.

To my annoyance, Margot answers.

'Hello, Margot, it's Daisy. Hope everything's okay. Can I say goodnight to the children please?'

'They're both tucked up in bed, all settled for the night.'

I glance at my watch. 'It's early for them to be asleep.'

'I don't think it's a good idea to unsettle them, Daisy. Everything is absolutely fine. You really must stop worrying. I did a perfectly good job in raising Haydn and I'm quite capable of caring for my grandchildren.'

'Is he there?'

'You mean Haydn, my son?'

I roll my eyes. She's always so obtuse. 'Yes.'

'The lovely boy is cooking me a delicious dinner. I'll go and see if he can be disturbed.'

I grit my teeth as I hear the clip-clop of her heels. Eventually she passes the phone to Haydn.

'Hi, love, are you having a good time?'

'Yes, fine, thanks. Is everything alright at home?'

'Hunky dory. The kids are fine, tucked up in bed and I'm cooking supper. They both had a good day at school. Mum's been amazing so there's nothing to worry about.'

'Alright,' I say hesitantly because I don't want to say goodbye to him. 'Send Ollie and Millie a big kiss from me and tell them I miss them. Have you got their games kitbags ready for tomorrow?'

'Of course. Your list is pinned on the fridge. We can manage, you know!' He laughs and it makes me feel a bit unwanted and unneeded. 'And before you ask, all the doors and windows are locked and Mum has even cleaned the house and ironed the sheets. Now off you go and have a lovely, relaxing time.'

'Okay, thanks, love,' I say, somewhat begrudgingly. 'I love you.'

'Love you too.' And then he's gone. I hand the phone back to Jenny.

'Nothing to worry about?' she asks, her head tilted to one side. I can tell that Jenny doesn't have children. There's always something to worry about when you have kids.

'All fine, thanks.' *For now*, I think.

I DON'T FEEL like being sociable so I meander back to my room. Exhaustion is really catching up with me and for the first time since I can remember, I'm looking forward to going to bed and falling asleep. It actually seems like the welcoming blackness of sleep could be in my grasp.

I slip under the smooth sheets and turn to switch the lights off, but neither of the switches on the wall do a thing. The bedside lamps are on and they won't switch off either. This is ridiculous. Have they set the lights so I can't switch them off? Last night I couldn't turn them on. I pull one of the bedside tables forward to get to the plug socket and see that the lamps have been hardwired into the wall.

I'm angry now. No, more than angry. This is like playing horrible mind games with people who are paying serious money to come on a retreat – although not, of course, in my case. Surely this can't be legal and it's certainly not humane. Isn't this torture?

I look around for a telephone to call reception but of course there isn't one.

Now I'm seething.

I stomp to the door, yank it open, let it swing hard behind me and march down the corridor, ready to bite off Jenny's head. Just as I'm rounding the corner, Amity appears. She's wearing a thick black jacket with a pale-blue scarf wrapped around her neck.

'Ah, Daisy. I was just coming to see you. Is everything alright?'

'No, it's not.' I put my hands on my waist. 'I would like to go to sleep and the lights won't switch off and I wanted to call reception for help but there is no phone. I can't imagine that any of that is legal and must certainly breach health and safety regulations.'

Amity laughs. She actually laughs, a surprisingly high-pitched, quite contagious tinkle. She puts a manicured hand on my arm. 'Come on, Daisy. Let's go back to your room and I'll show you how everything works.'

What? Why didn't she explain everything to me when I first got here?

In my room, she slides open the bedside table drawer and inside is a little white plastic box with a knob on it. 'All you need to do is press that and it calls straight through to reception. That triggers the two-way intercom and then you can speak aloud your request and we can answer you. Otherwise the intercom is strictly one way, to preserve your privacy of course. I did show you this when we did our induction,' she says gently.

I stare at her, because she most certainly did not. There is no way I'd forget being told that I can't control the lights and that there is an intercom through which instructions will be beamed into my room with no warning. It's like having Big Brother in the bedroom with me and it sends a shiver down my spine.

'All of this was explicitly stated in the documents you signed when you arrived,' she presses. 'I'm happy to show you copies if you like.'

Or did she tell me? Half the time I forget things, but something like this I know I wouldn't have forgotten. I'm positive I would have walked straight out.

'Please don't worry, Daisy. It's all totally above board. We follow very strict procedures, all of the ISO standards are exceeded and we have regular inspections by the Health and Safety Executive and Health Protection Agency. My only concern is the wellbeing of my clients. Besides, I'm hardly going to put a foot out of line when I'm caring for a journalist!

My methods are a little different but as you'll see by the end of the week, they actually work.'

I suppose she's right. She couldn't possibly risk doing anything illegal with me here. I'll just write about it and that could destroy her business.

I take a deep breath.

'Tonight it's all about sleep deprivation.' She pauses to gauge my reaction. 'Oh, Daisy! The look on your face. It's nothing to worry about. As I said before, unfortunately there's no gain without pain. Yes, it might be hard for a few hours but it will be totally worth it when your sleeplessness is banished forever. I want you to dance this evening. Move to the music, enjoy yourself. Imagine you're twenty again, in a night club having a fantastic time. Remember how it felt when you were utterly exhausted but you still kept going because you were enjoying yourself so much. That's the feeling you're going to capture tonight. You'll have to excuse me now because I've got to get back to my husband and kids, but have a good night and I'll see you in the morning.'

I watch Amity leave the room. Is this woman real or is this all some horrible human experiment? I think about the spa and how it's all set up. The furniture is so luxurious, the food is delicious and the staff are lovely. No, this has to be the real deal. It's just my exhaustion making me doubt things.

I sit back down on the bed and then the music starts. It's not just any music, but songs from my late teens and early twenties, the hits of the day, the music I used to bop to in dingy nightclubs in Brighton. And then the lights start flickering and changing colour, moving to the beat of the music. This is crazy! I can't decide whether to laugh or cry. I wish Haydn was here with me. Neither of us are great dancers but we would laugh together, perhaps pretend to recapture the moves from our youth. Instead, I'm all alone and I have no wish to dance. I just want to sleep.

The music is loud and I'm wondering if it's gradually getting louder. I climb into bed and pull two pillows over my head, jamming my hands over them to try to reduce the sound in my ears. But I still hear the *thump thump* of the beat and feel the vibrations through the bed. There is no way I'm going to be able to sleep through this. It goes on. And on. And on. The lights continue to change colour and flicker in time with the beats. This is insane.

I take out the journal that Amity gave me and I write in it. Fat, forceful words that mark the paper in frustration.

My thoughts on The Serinity Spa: This place is deluxe but it's not for the faint-hearted. Whether Amity Augustiago's therapy sessions and hypnosis, combined with health analyses and massages actually cure my insomnia remains to be seen. But right now I am SO ANGRY I WANT TO SCREAM. There is loud music playing in my bedroom and dazzling lights; it's like torture. In fact it is bloody torture. Isn't this what they do to prisoners to break them? I want to break...

And then I do.

I try to snap the pen in half but all that happens is it flies across the room and I find myself sobbing. I feel like I'm going mad. The music plays on and on. I go into the bathroom and turn the shower on full blast. At least the water drowns out some of the sound but now the fear hits again. What if something terrible is happening at home? Haydn is such a deep sleeper, would he smell smoke if the house was burning? And what about me?

My head feels as if it's going to explode and I wonder if I'm going insane. I'm still sobbing as I switch the water off and towel dry. I want to go home, to feel Haydn's arms around me, to kiss the soft cheeks of my children. If I wasn't so bone-weary exhausted, I'd get in my car right now and drive home. This is torture and I don't care if The Serinity Spa gets ten out of ten for it's methods and best practice, I cannot do this any more.

It's 1:30 am when I stomp back into the bedroom, pull open my bedside table drawer and jam my hand down on the button.

A few seconds later the music stops.

It's a male voice. 'How can I help?'

'You need to stop the bloody music and lights. It's horrific. Tell Amity it's got to stop, and I don't give a toss if you call her and wake her up in the middle of the night.' I'm shocked at my own language. I hardly ever swear.

'Of course, Mrs McKenzie. I'm sorry it is making you so distressed. I'll switch everything off immediately. I hope you have a good night and don't hesitate to call me again if you need anything.'

Then the room is plunged into darkness and silence and all I'm left with are the incessant thoughts bouncing around inside my head.

9

It's 6:30 am and breakfast time when I stride into the dining room. To my annoyance, Daisy isn't here. She simply can't be allowed to lounge around in the mornings, because we have an end game and a tight timetable which I intend to keep. I march down the corridor to her room and rap on the door, loudly. I could have used the intercom but I want to look into her eyes this morning.

I knock again. Eventually, I hear the shuffle of footsteps and the door opens.

'Goodness, Daisy, are you alright?' She looks terrible. She has purple-grey rings under her bloodshot eyes, her hair is lank, yet messy and her face pale. Seeing her in such a state, being subjected to such a brutal treatment programme, I'm in danger of feeling sorry for her, but I remind myself that neither empathy nor sympathy are deserved.

'Not really. I don't think I slept a wink last night. I'm not sure this course, or whatever it is is working for me.'

'Oh, Daisy,' I say, stepping into the room and letting the door close behind me. 'It is totally understandable that you're feeling this way. I did too when I went through the programme. It's hell for the first couple of days and nights, absolute hell. But you'll look back on these days as the time when you broke the cycle. It's the only way I'm afraid. We're taking a two-pronged approach with you, shocking your body into exhaustion and uncovering the root of the problem through an assessment of your mind. Today we'll go deeper into the reasons for your sleeplessness. I wish I could make this process easier for you, I really do. Tell me, what's your favourite food for breakfast?'

She thinks for a very long time and eventually says, 'Pancakes.'

'In which case I'll get chef to make you some. Have a nice shower and then come down to the dining room. Breakfast will be ready in half an hour.'

I WATCH Daisy discretely as she eats her breakfast and I'm shocked by how weak she appears, how her hand shakes as she barely manages to get her fork into her mouth. I wonder whether I should get Doctor Dhingra to give her a once over, but then decide no. I'm not going to waste his valuable time on her unnecessarily. I go to my private room and find a bottle of supplements – they're placebos in fact, nothing in them except some cornflour and sugar – and I pop two inside a little paper cup. I then walk back to the dining room, to Daisy's table.

'We're going to give you some special supplements to help you stay awake today so that tonight you'll have the best sleep of your life.'

Daisy's reaction is slow. I can see she's trying to formulate a response but the exhaustion is beating any coherent thoughts. I'm both pleased and surprised at how quickly my plan is working.

'Just swallow these supplements with a glass of juice or

water. When you've finished breakfast, I've booked you in for a wonderfully relaxing head and hand massage using aromatherapy oils.' I see her flinch slightly and I suppose she's thinking about the brutal massage she had yesterday. 'Nothing like yesterday,' I say, trying to reassure her. 'This is truly glorious. Afterwards, we'll do a session of hypnosis.' I lean over to pat her hand but then pull away at the last moment. I don't want to touch her. 'Please don't worry, Daisy, you'll be feeling better very soon.'

This is all part of my plan. This morning I want Daisy to be calm and in a truly relaxed frame of mind so I can work my magic through hypnosis. That is my best hope for success.

HALF AN HOUR LATER, while Daisy is having her Indian head massage, I take the opportunity to go to her room. I make sure that none of the housekeeping staff are around and I slip inside using my master key.

The bedroom has been made up and Daisy's belongings are neatly stored away in the wardrobe. I go through everything: every drawer, cupboard, and check under the bed. I look inside her empty suitcase, in her handbag and her washbag, and only when I'm one hundred per cent sure there are no hidden phones or electronic devices do I truly relax. I wasn't expecting to find anything as it's not like she knew in advance of coming here that we have a no-device policy, but she is a journalist and even if she's only writing for some ridiculous second-rate magazine, she'll have a nose for a story. I'm not naive enough to think that the lust for uncovering the truth ever goes away.

Next, I have a look through her things to try to find out more about Daisy. She has a sweet photograph of her husband – who is rather good looking – and her two young children propped up against the bedside light. Her washbag doesn't reveal anything I don't already know. She has sleeping pills – melatonin and over-the-counter painkillers – but nothing else. I read what she has scrawled in her journal and when I see *I am SO ANGRY I WANT TO SCREAM*, I laugh. *You're going to want to do more than scream*, I think. Also she hasn't really taken on board my advice for her to journal her thoughts properly. I'll need to do something about that. All in all, it's rather a disappointment.

I slip back to my treatment room unnoticed, not that any of the staff would think anything untoward if they saw me coming out of a guest room. This is my spa after all and sometimes I have to pinch myself to remember that this is my vision, my success story, and the only help I got was the financial backing from Keith. But that's what spouses are for: if they can help each other, then they should.

An hour later and Daisy is in my therapy room, looking so much better than she did at breakfast.

'Did you enjoy the massage?' I ask.

She leans her head back in the armchair. 'It was glorious, exactly what I needed. Thank you.'

I've made her an herbal tea which I pass across the coffee table.

'I'm glad to see the supplements are having a positive effect on you. So today I'd like to talk to you about aversion therapy. Do you know what that is?'

'It's when someone is addicted to something and you help them associate something negative with that addiction so they give it up.'

'Exactly. I'd like to give you an example. I had a young client who'd developed an irrational phobia about eating fruit and vegetables. This young man simply wouldn't eat them and it was affecting his health. So under hypnosis I told him to imagine a beautiful, dark starry night, with a large, round moon and to visualise the moon as a round, white cabbage, about to be shredded and cooked in butter. I told him the sky is black, the deep, rich colour of black, juicy grapes, so sweet and moreish. As the sun comes up I told him to imagine it was a big, ripe tomato bursting with flavour on his tongue. During this relaxation, we associated delightful things with the ordinary. After three sessions, this young man overcame his aversion to fruit and veg and was eating normally. Now you, Daisy, have developed an irrational fear about sleep. You've come to associate your bed and bedtime with a fear of the consequences a lack of sleep brings. Your body is in a constant, heightened state and full of inflammation, due to a prolonged period of unrest. I'd like to try a similar hypnosis on you to eliminate that fear so that when you next go to bed, you will be looking forward to falling asleep. You will associate it with wondrous relaxation. What do you think?'

'Um, yes, I suppose it makes sense. I didn't think I feared going to bed but I suppose I'm always worried I won't sleep. It's like right now, I'd love to go to bed. I feel exhausted and drowsy.'

'Yes, but now it's the morning and not the appropriate time for you to sleep. I want you to feel like this at night-time.' I smile because that's exactly how I hoped she'd be feeling. Relaxed, open and suggestive. Daisy is no fool, and I need to play her very carefully.

'Lie down on the daybed, Daisy, please.' I drop a blanket over her, making sure I don't touch her.

'Are you comfortable?' I ask, as I settle back into my chair.

'Yes, thank you.'

Then I dim the lights right down, no colours today. I talk her through the initial relaxation stage, easing the tension in her muscles, walking her down the stairs to her special place. Her breathing is slow and steady.

'Daisy, bring the index finger of your right hand to touch the tip of your nose.'

Her eyes are firmly closed but she does as I say. That's good because she's in a perfect state of relaxation, but it's not good enough for today's work. I need to work through an additional script, one that I very rarely use, to bring on amnesia. It's a more complicated script with language that sounds nonsensical, all designed to make my subject forget everything that I am about to say. I go carefully and slowly, taking her to the very edge of sleep, and only when I'm totally confident that Daisy is in the perfect state of relaxation do I finally begin.

'Daisy,' I say in a soft and steady voice – which belies my excitement and the fast beating of my heart. 'When you feel tired and go to bed, sleep won't come. Whenever you hear the word bed, adrenaline will pump through your body and you will feel terror. You must not allow sleep. Sleep is your enemy, Daisy. You must stay awake. You *must* stay awake. When I count one, two, three and you awake, you won't remember anything I just said. You won't worry about sleep, but when you get to your bed, the fear will return. You won't know why but your brain will work hard to keep you awake.' I pause for a moment to make sure that Daisy is still in a hypnotic state. She is lying there on the daybed, her mouth slightly open, so vulnerable and weak it disgusts me. If she was any other client, I might pull the blanket up to cover her more, but this is Daisy and even being in the same room as her fills me with utter revulsion.

Poor, poor Daisy. She won't remember a word of this and rather than her sleep improving, it's going to get dramatically worse. Of course I need to drill down into Daisy's specific fears to make this truly effective, but that will happen. We still have several days.

I then bring her back to wakefulness.

'How was that, Daisy?' I ask, as I turn the lights back up to full strength and slide the blind up to let the sunlight enter the room.

'I feel like I had a really deep sleep.'

'That's what good hypnosis feels like. Deeply relaxing but also very refreshing,' I say, as I scribble some notes on this session. 'And do you remember anything we talked about during your hypnosis?' I try to keep my voice casual.

'No, it's weird. I remember the tone of your voice but I can't recall a single word you said.'

'That's perfectly normal and a sign that it's working. Great news.' I swivel around and glance at my watch. 'It's nearly time for lunch, so why don't you go and have a lovely lunch and then take an hour's rest in the meditation room. After that I'd like you to spend half an hour in the sauna. Later this afternoon we'll have another session where we'll go deeper into exploring the root causes of your sleeplessness. How does that sound?'

Daisy stretches her arms above her head. 'Sounds great. Thank you so much for all of this,' she says.

I hand her a printout of today's programme. 'If we can sort out your problems and you write a lovely article on The Serenity Spa, then we'll both be winners,' I say with a saccharine smile.

Oh, Daisy, poor, poor Daisy. You have no idea what you've let yourself in for. Sleep is like pseudo death but permanent wakefulness can kill you.

10

DAISY

For the first time that I can remember I feel rested. My limbs are languid and it's hard to wipe the grin off my face. I have no idea what Amity's magic is, but for now it's working. Hope. That's what she's given me, and hope leads to happiness.

As I float into the dining room, I see that Flo is back. Her shoulders are hunched and she looks miserable. Rosemary waves at me maniacally and I give a little flutter of my fingers in return.

'Hey, what's up?' I ask Flo as I sit at our table.

'It's the burglary. Amity let me speak to Si because the burglary is a police matter. He told me they stole our wedding rings that he'd had engraved and I know they cost him a fortune, but it's not the money, it's our wedding rings and I'm worried it's an omen. I mean we're not even married yet and they took the two items that mean the most. The police have no leads. Si says they don't seem the slightest bit bothered. I'm not even sure I want to go home now; it's like the place has been violated. You know what I mean?'

'I'm so sorry, Flo, but don't look at it as an omen. It's just bad luck and unfortunately these things happen. There's time for Si to buy new rings and I assume you're covered by insurance?'

'Yeah, it's not the money, it's just horrible.'

The waitress brings over a plate piled high with food for me and a bowl of clear broth for Flo. She stares at my chicken breast and rice with eyes of longing. I feel for her. It seems cruel for me to be eating heartily while she goes hungry. I wonder if I should say something to Amity, but then Flo's scooping her spoon into her broth and she starts talking about her wedding again. I interject with the occasional platitude but really I'm not listening. Flo's a sweet girl and I'm sorry that this happened to her but I'm too busy enjoying the meal and the sense of relaxation from my hypnotherapy that makes my body feel heavy. It isn't until I'm eating a fine strawberry tart that I realise Flo's talk of burglary hasn't triggered me to feel fearful. Of course the moment I think that the worry returns. I try to be rational; it's daytime now and Margot will be at home and the children safely at school.

After lunch, I climb into a hanging pod in the meditation room. My body feels lethargic and my mind calm. The windows are wide open and the sun warms the room, making it feel as if I'm in a hammock being rocked gently by the wind, and I listen to the rolling waves of the ocean. It's so comfortable here that I wonder if I'll sleep or at least doze but every time my eyelids close something awakens me: a squawking seagull in the distance, voices from the room next door, the breeze whispering over my face. It's frustrating. Even so, I lose track of time.

I jump when Jenny appears in front of me. 'Sorry to disturb you, Daisy, but it's time for your session in the sauna.' I clamber out of the pod inelegantly and with some difficulty, then follow Jenny. We walk downstairs to the treatment corridor, past closed doors and then she opens a door signed *Bathroom*.

'You can have a shower in here,' she says, showing me a communal changing area. 'The sauna is the next door down on the right. Strip off and just wear a towel around you or go naked – whatever you prefer. Amity says you shouldn't stay in there for more than thirty minutes.'

'Thanks,' I say.

I've only been in a sauna once before and I didn't enjoy it. They make me feel hot, sweaty and claustrophobic but I know they're good for me, so I'm prepared to give this a go.

After a quick shower, I wrap a white fluffy towel around my torso and open the sauna door. What I wasn't expecting was to have to share it. Naive of me perhaps as this is a wellness facility for all the guests, but there are two women inside who are completely naked, leaning backwards, exposed, totally carefree. One of them looks up at me, smiles briefly, flicking her long hair backwards, and carries on talking to her friend. These women are beautiful, perfectly proportioned and frankly look like models. And then there's me. I sit to one side, as far away from them as possible. There is no way I'm letting my towel go, however hot this place gets; I'm keeping my modesty.

It gets hot very quickly and I can feel a layer of sweat building up. Everything is sticky and I'm sure my face is red. After a couple of minutes, the two women get up and leave, nodding at me as they strut out the door, not even bothering to cover themselves with their towels as they go. Oh to have such confidence... but I'm relieved I'm alone now. I release the grip on my towel simply because it's too damn hot.

But then, just a few seconds later, the sauna door opens again and in comes Rosemary. My heart sinks. I pull the towel up to cover myself but she takes one look at me and laughs.

'Don't be shy on my account,' she says. She shuts the door behind her and proceeds to sit on the same bench as me, so close we're almost touching. Rosemary lets her towel fall away and I do everything I can to avert my eyes.

'I've never been in a sauna before,' she says. 'It's terribly hot, isn't it?'

I nod.

'So how are you doing, Daisy? Did you sleep last night?'

'I don't mean to be rude, Rosemary,' I say, as I try to shift as discretely as possible away from her. 'But I'd like to do some meditation whilst I'm in here.'

'What together?' she asks.

'No. Just in my head, in silence.'

'Oh, I see.' She goes quiet and she's probably taken offence. Then she says, 'I don't know much about saunas but I think I'm going to boil like a lobster.'

We sit quietly for perhaps a minute and then all of a sudden she stands up.

'Think I'm going to faint,' she says, the forced tone of her voice suggesting the opposite. She wraps the towel around her. 'You enjoy yourself in here but the sauna isn't for me.' Her face is beetroot red and there's sweat dripping down her forehead and plastering her hair to her forehead.

'Bye,' I say quietly, at last relaxing my back against the wall now that I'm in here alone. I'm not sure how long I sit there feeling more and more uncomfortable, sweat dripping down my body, thinking Rosemary was sensible to leave so quickly. It feels like my throat is closing up and my nostrils are burning, almost as if the hot, dry air is choking me, setting my lungs on fire. This is horrid and I need to leave. I hold the towel around myself, stand up and walk to the door. I push it.

Nothing happens.

I try again, but still it doesn't budge. Could Rosemary

have locked me in by mistake? The heat is making me feel dizzy and now claustrophobia kicks in. The walls seem to melt towards me, sweat is pouring down my forehead, into my eyes, dripping into every crevasse of my body. I need to get out of here!

Stay calm, I tell myself. *You must be trying to open the door wrongly.* I try it again, lifting up the latch to release the door, but still it doesn't budge. And now the panic sets in.

Surely I haven't been locked in the sauna? How long until someone notices that I'm missing? Will I survive that long?

I bang on the door and scream for help. But my hands are slippery and all I'm doing is hurting myself. I use my shoulder, bruising it as I bang it against the wood, but it makes no difference. This door is solid cedar.

'Help!' I scream. 'Help!'

It's so hard to breathe in here, and the more I gulp the less air I seem to be taking in. Rosemary must have wedged the door on her way out. Did I upset her and this is her revenge? No, that's ridiculous; I'm catastrophising as usual.

Time warps and I have no idea how long I've been shouting for. My voice is hoarse and my is heart thudding so fast I wonder if I'm going to have a heart attack. And then suddenly, the door swings open and wonderful, cool air floods in.

'Mrs McKenzie, are you alright?' Jenny asks.

'Of course I'm not bloody alright!' I say, almost falling out of the sauna as I push my way past her, clutching my towel to stop it from falling down. 'I was locked in! It locked me in! How is that even possible?'

Jenny pales, a look of shock on her pretty face. 'It's not possible,' she says quietly.

'Well it is!' I shout. I can't help myself; the sheer panic gives way to tears. 'I'm not an idiot. I know how to open a door. There's something wrong with the latch.' And then I feel really bad. This isn't Jenny's fault, she's only trying to help.

'Sometimes the latch is a little sticky,' she says, demonstrating how it lifts up and down. 'Maybe there's a bit of a technique.' Her voice fades away and I realise she's only trying to be empathetic. I watch as she removes her shoes and walks into the sauna. She shuts the door behind herself, even though she's fully dressed, and a second later the door opens and she comes out. I suppose it was me in my desperate panic, my fingers slipping, my brain not functioning properly. I sink onto a wooden bench in the changing area, trying to stop my hands from trembling, failing to get my rapid breathing under control.

'I think you might have had a panic attack,' Jenny says. I know she's trying to be helpful but it's not what I need to hear. What I really need is a big glass of brandy to calm the nerves, except they don't serve spirits here.

'When you've had a shower, Amity will see you. I'm sure she'll be able to calm you down.'

That's just what I don't feel like, another interrogation by Amity.

THE FRUSTRATING THING is that all of that wonderful calmness I felt earlier has dissipated and now I'm tense, with exhaustion gnawing at my limbs and snaking through my veins. It's not that delicious, relaxed tiredness that I felt earlier, but a terror that starts deep in my belly and spreads up to my throat. It's not helped by the fact that Amity has made it perfectly clear she wants to delve into when and why my insomnia started. I just hope my brain is sufficiently alert to stop myself from saying too much.

'Daisy, Daisy,' Amity says, walking towards me with her arms outstretched. 'I hear you had a horrible experience in the sauna. I'm so dreadfully sorry. One of our maintenance team is looking at the door now to make sure it never happens again. It must have been terrifying for you and please accept my apologies.'

'Thanks,' I say softly. Amity must be worried that I might write something about it in my piece. I won't; these things happen and I'm not proud of how I reacted.

'Have a seat,' she says. 'I made you a special brew of calming tea.'

I flop into the armchair and shiver slightly, although it's not cold in here. Amity hands me a fawn mohair throw and I wrap it around myself.

'This afternoon we're going to explore what might have started your sleeplessness, and try to clear any suppression or repression of painful or difficult memories. This session will be just like we're having a chat and it will last for an hour or so. Last time we spoke, you told me how much you enjoyed your job as a young journalist and you shared your dream of working for a broadsheet. I know you're working for a London glossy magazine now, but did the big journalism dream ever get fulfilled?'

'No.' I sigh.

'What happened?'

I pause while I consider how much to tell Amity. 'Things just didn't work out the way I'd dreamed.'

'There is always a trigger or a reason why our dreams aren't fulfilled. It can be an event that sends us off in a new direction, self-doubt or self-sabotage for instance. What was the catalyst in your case?' Amity asks.

'Things changed after I was assigned to report on a court case.'

'Tell me more about it,' she prompts. I realise that there is little point in me continuing this programme if I don't give

Amity at least a heavily edited version of events. I inhale deeply and start talking.

'It wasn't the first court case I was assigned to, but for some reason this one really got to me. It was held at The Royal Courts of Justice on The Strand in London, a high profile case, and I was one of many journalists jostling for a seat in the public gallery. It was a murder trial for the brutal stabbing of a young man in what seemed to be a random attack. I know it's a common occurrence these days, but fifteen years ago knife crime wasn't quite as prevalent. The defendant was a nasty piece of work.'

'What happened?'

'The trial went on for a fortnight and I was there every day, soaking up all of the gory detail. It turns out the victim wasn't the innocent young lad the prosecution made him out to be. He was a member of a rival gang and had probably been treading on rival turf. He still didn't deserve to die.'

'Of course not. So what was it about this case that got to you?'

I look away from Amity. I do not want to be having this conversation, not now, not at any time. I've worked very hard to bury the past. I'm exhausted, emotional and all I want to do is go to bed, ideally with Haydn at my side.

Amity tilts her head, her eyes open wide, her expression warm.

'I'm sorry, but I don't want to go into it,' I tell her.

'I realise this might be painful for you, Daisy, but by exploring what happened is the only way we're going to rid you of your sleeplessness for good. I also want to reassure you that everything you say in this room is confidential. The thing is, unless you're honest with yourself, you're never going to be cured. Does that make sense?'

I nod reluctantly.

'I've never told anyone, not even my husband.' My voice is nearly a whisper.

Amity reaches across and moves as if she's going to take my hand. She pauses for a moment and I wonder whether it's unethical to physically touch a client. But then she holds my hand in hers ever so gently. Her palm is cool and soft and she holds my hand with such a lightness of touch, as if it has great fragility. 'The only way to a cure is honesty. I've taken an oath of confidentiality. Nothing you say in this room will ever be repeated. If I did that, I would no longer be allowed to practice.'

I pull my hand away, sit back and briefly close my eyes. I suppose I should trust Amity because what have I got to lose? She wants me to write a good review on this place and I need help.

There. I said it aloud, in my head at least. I need help. Is it possible that Amity might be my saviour after nearly fifteen years of insomnia hell? Of course she's not going to tell anyone. She's like a doctor, sworn to secrecy.

'What are you thinking, Daisy?'

'What if I tell you something that is illegal? What would you do?'

'The only time I would ever break a client's confidentiality is if I believe my client or someone else is at risk of imminent physical harm from themselves or by others.'

I nod because I already know this. Of course she's not going to tell the authorities what I tell her. Perhaps I will feel better if I share the words... words that I have never uttered to anyone, even Haydn. Especially Haydn. How could I tell him now after we've been together for so long?

'It was something that happened at that murder trial, I assume?' Amity prompts.

'Yes. One day during a recess I was followed into the court toilets. I was in a cubicle minding my own business when a voice from an adjacent cubicle said, "Hey, journalist, you should investigate jury influencers in the Kyle case." It was a woman speaking with a deep voice and a poor attempt at an American accent. I hesitated. Was that nugget of information for me? I assumed so. I dashed out of the toilet just a few seconds later, but there was no one else there. Not a soul in any of the cubicles. I ran outside to the corridor, which was packed with people milling between courts. I didn't even know what jury influencing was at that stage, I was so young and naive.'

'You think you were targeted?'

'I'm sure I was. Young, female, innocent, working for a big paper. Perfect prey. And most of all I was hungry for a good story. Someone wanted the truth to be told and thought I would be the perfect conduit. My ambition was over-whelming in those days and I wondered if this could be my big break. I didn't tell any of my colleagues what I'd been told, not even my boss. I wanted to investigate this one myself and potentially reap massive rewards.'

I pause and take a sip of the herbal tea which is now cold.

'So you investigated and what did you find?'

'I started following members of the jury. I'd follow them from the courts all the way to their homes, even watching them when they went to the shops or went out to the pub in the evenings. I started with the young guys. There were three of them, ranging from early twenties to mid-thirties, but the more I dug into their lives the more normal they seemed. It appeared I was barking up the wrong tree. The next person I shadowed was the jury spokesperson. If I'd been older and wiser I might have started with him because I guess he had the most influence. But he seemed respectable, mid-forties, married with three kids, and lived in Acton in one of those mock-Tudor houses. I learned a good lesson; banish your preconceived ideas and stereotypes. I saw something suspicious.' I swallow, but it's as if something is wedged in my throat and my epiglottis has got stuck. Amity pours me a glass of water and slides it across the table.

'What did you see?'

'It was after a day in court. I followed the jury spokesperson to the tube, sat a few seats down from him and then followed as he changed tubes. When he exited the station at Acton this other guy appeared. He was wearing jeans, a black hoodie and a beanie that he'd pulled down low. He stood at a strange angle, his back to the street, out of view of any security cameras – and of course there weren't as many cameras around back then as there are today. Anyway, he sidled up to the jury spokesperson and handed him a padded envelope. They spoke a few words which I couldn't hear and the spokesperson glanced around before shoving the envelope into his inside jacket pocket. It looked so dodgy but it didn't prove anything, so I just carried on following the jury spokesperson. And then I was sure that I saw the beanie guy in the public gallery the next day. I mean I couldn't be absolutely sure, but I had that feeling.

'It happened again three days later just outside Acton station. The beanie guy handed over an envelope, all suspicious, and this time I felt I had to say something, do something. I was about to march up to the spokesperson and demand to know what was in the envelope but beanie guy must have spotted me.'

'What happened then?' Amity asks.

'I walked out of the station following the jury spokesperson at quite a distance. I had no idea that beanie guy was following me, but obviously he was. He waited until the street was empty of people and cars and then a strong, wiry arm circled my waist and his hot rancid breath was in my ear. '"You didn't see nothing," he said. "You open that pretty little mouth of yours and you'll be dead next. No more snooping, no stories, no lawyers, no police. Get it?" 'I was absolutely terrified. "Go home," he said. And I did. I turned around and bolted back to the station.'

'You think the man in the beanie was bribing the jury spokesperson?' Amity asks. Her eyes are wide and she's so far forward on her seat it looks like she's going to fall off.

'I don't think so, I'm sure. They call it jury nobbling. He knew exactly who I was and what I suspected, and I was terrified.'

'Oh, Daisy, that's awful.'

I glance at my hands. My fingers are curled into tight balls. What I can't tell Amity is that Aaron Sullivan – because years later I found out that was beanie guy's name – has never gone away. He sends me reminders every year or so; a weird note in the post; following me and standing too close to me on the train; the burglary at home. The last time I saw him, he was loitering outside the children's school gates, just long enough for me to see him as if to say: I know where you live, I know where your kids go to school, I know everything about you, Daisy McKenzie, so if you open your mouth, I'll get you and your family. I tremble just thinking about him. And what's worse, I haven't seen or heard from Aaron in over eighteen months and I'm terrified of what his next reminder might be. Because it's time. I know he hasn't been sent to prison again because I keep an eye out for that. All I can hope is that he's moved abroad or he's dead. And that's why I don't sleep because I can't be sure of what Aaron might do next.

'What happened in the trial?' Amity asks.

'He got off. The man who was on trial for murder got off and it was my fault because I wasn't brave enough to say anything about the jury nobbling. I could have gone to the police or told my boss, but I was too scared, too much of a wimp.'

'How old were you?'

'Twenty-three,' I say.

'So young,' Amity murmurs. 'And you never told anyone about this?'

I shake my head.

'Oh, Daisy, it's totally understandable why this would be eating you up. But you were so young and inexperienced and it's not like it was your fault that the jury found him not guilty.'

'But it was,' I say, swiping away my tears with the back of my hand.

'This happened such a long time ago, I'm wondering why it's still bothering you?' she asks. 'Let's talk some more about it.'

'No. I've said enough. I don't want to think about it.'

'Unfortunately the brain doesn't work like that, Daisy. You need to articulate what happened, your fears and why it's affecting your sleep. Tell me more.'

I shake my head. I've said quite enough, too much. It's exhausting sharing my story and I don't want to tell Amity any more.

'I'm tired,' I say. That's the understatement of the year.

Amity looks pensive for a moment and then says, 'Maybe it'll be easier for you to write it down if you're not comfortable talking about it. It's eating away at you, how you've buried these events and tried to forget about them, but your subconscious mind doesn't forget. Writing about experiences can be very cathartic and I suspect it will help you enormously.'

I'm not so sure. 'Will I have to show it to you?'

Amity pulls her head back and looks shocked. 'Absolutely not. What you write in your journal is confidential. That journal is for your eyes only.'

That's a relief. Perhaps it's worth giving it a go on the basis that I can burn the journal when I get home.

'I think that's probably enough for today as you look exhausted. I'm very pleased with your progress. How are you feeling now?'

'A bit better,' I say, because it's true. I do feel a little lighter. I might have only shared a small portion of my story, but it's a relief to think that by speaking it out aloud, I could be taking my first step to achieving a proper night's sleep.

11

DAISY

I return to my room and sink onto the comfortable bed with a sense of relief. I've tried so hard not to think about the court case and specifically what happened later, but now it's brought back all the memories. What if Aaron turns up at home while I'm not there? What if he tries to do something to the children; what would Margot do? Such thoughts make my heart beat too fast and my breathing becomes shallow. I sit up and the room spins. I can't catch my breath. I panic more. Are my lungs closing up? Am I going to die alone, here in this lovely room?

I dig a nail into my thigh and try to pull myself together. This is the beginning of a panic attack and I must remember to breathe slowly. In and out.

There's a knock on my door and I ignore it. It comes again. I swing my legs out of bed, pull the dressing gown tightly around my waist and open the door. It's only now I realise there's no peephole in the door like there is in most hotels.

My heart sinks when I see Rosemary.

'I heard the news that you got locked in the sauna. Just wanted to check you're alright.'

'I'm fine, thank you.' I wonder who told her. I can't imagine it was Jenny who seems the very model of discretion.

'I smuggled in a little bottle of brandy, you know, just in case. I wondered if you'd like a little swig just to calm the nerves.'

That's exactly what I would like but instead I shake my head. 'Thanks, but I won't.'

'I was also wondering if I could pick your brains about some of the insomnia cures you've tried. I only got three hours sleep last night despite the glorious massages yesterday. Can I come in?'

She takes a step towards me and I automatically step backwards, and before I know it, Rosemary is in my bedroom.

'Oh, this is lovely!' she says, clapping her hands together. 'I was a late booking, so my room looks onto the back not the sea.' She walks towards the window and from behind, her frizzy-grey hair creates a halo around her head. When she turns around to face me, there are tears in her eyes.

'My life isn't sorted like yours, Daisy. You've got such an important job and what you say and do affects so many people. I'm in total admiration of you.'

The walls seem to draw in closer; I've never experienced this full-on fan-girl-type behaviour before and it makes me extremely uncomfortable.

'And look at you; you're wearing no makeup and your hair is all mussed up but you still look beautiful. Just give me one little tip how to make my life more like yours!' She forces her mouth into a smile but a tear drips from her left eye, down her cheek and onto the floor. I don't know what to say to Rosemary because she is so very wrong. My life isn't sorted; I have insomnia; I'm not a good mum and I'm in danger of losing my job, which means my family will lose their home.

'Um, I don't know,' I say.

She shakes her head. 'And you're modest too.' She moves to the end of the bed and sits down, then pats the space next to her. 'Come and sit with me. I want to know when your insomnia started. Mine was when I got jilted. I was just eighteen and meant to marry my childhood sweetheart but he didn't turn up at the church. He told me he got cold feet but two months later he was married to someone else. They've got five children now and three grandchildren. Can you imagine? I haven't met anyone else. Facebook is lovely, isn't it, because it helps you stay in touch with people so easily.'

I stay standing. This poor woman hasn't got over having her heart broken. Assuming she's in her fifties or early sixties, that could be forty years of grieving, forty years of jealousy, forty years of desperation. I wonder whether she stalks her ex anywhere other than Facebook and whether he knows. I decide I don't wish to know. I glance at my watch.

'It's nearly time for supper. Shall we go together?'

She jumps up from the bed. 'A lovely idea, Daisy.'

As we walk into the small dining room, Rosemary makes a beeline for my table, but I'm relieved when the waitress intervenes.

'You're over here this evening, Rosemary,' she says with such a broad smile, Rosemary can't object. I wait for Flo to arrive but she doesn't appear. I can tell that Rosemary is aggrieved, being forced to sit with a young woman who studiously ignores her, when there's an empty chair at my table. I do my best not to catch Rosemary's eye. I hope Flo is alright but assume she's gone home. I wonder if she'll fit into her wedding dress after eating so little during her stay here. As I'm toying with my tomato soup, Amity startles me by slipping into the empty chair opposite. She leans across the table and talks in a hushed whisper.

'You did so well this afternoon, Daisy, but I'm giving you homework this evening. I want you to go back to your room after supper and write down everything about that court case that upset you and still upsets you. Don't leave a single thing out. Then I want you to write down the emotions you feel when you think about those memories. This isn't an easy exercise because you have been burying these feelings for years, but please give it a good go. Tomorrow we'll do hypnosis again, to banish the bad memories. Have a good night and I'll see you in the morning.'

'Thanks,' I say, but that's just me being polite. I have no desire to write everything down, no wish to think about the past. The only consolation is, it's better to write it down than speak it out aloud. Oh, there is another consolation: I now have the perfect excuse for not spending the evening with Rosemary. The thought makes me feel guilty but I'm here to focus on myself, not to act as a mentor and sounding board to a stranger.

THE NOTEBOOK IS beautiful and deserves to hold sweeping, cursive writing laid down with an old-fashioned ink pen, not the horrible scrawl that I wrote last night. Carefully, I tear that page out, rip it into little pieces and drop them into the rubbish bin. I notice that a new Serinity Spa pen has been placed next to my bed. I pick it up and start writing.

Aaron. I didn't know his name back then; that didn't come to light until a few years later.
He had dark hair and was clean shaven, probably late twenties. There was nothing particularly extraordinary about him, he was neither good looking nor unattractive.

Perhaps five feet ten inches, slender in build and the sort of person who could slip in and out of a room unnoticed. It was Aaron's eyes that were his most distinguishable feature: dark, deep set, the sort of eyes that never let go. They haunted me then and they still haunt me today. I shiver whenever I see anyone with deep-set eyes.

Every day after our unpleasant meeting at Acton station, he sat in the public gallery and stared at me. Whenever I glanced up he was looking in my direction; it was as if his eyes were permanently fixed on my face. When Kyle Franklin was found not guilty, he smiled at me, and I saw that he was missing several teeth on the left side of his jaw. It was a horrible grin that imprinted itself onto my memory. Worse was to come. As I left the courtroom and eased my way through the crowds in the corridor, he appeared right next to me and clutched my elbow. His fingers digging into my flesh, he whispered into my ear. 'Breathe a word and you're dead. And not just you. Your poor dad who's just lost his job and your mum who has breast cancer and your little sister who's about to graduate from Birmingham uni. Remember.' And then he vanished. I rushed to the toilets and threw up. I was that scared. But what could I do? My window of opportunity for sharing what I knew had gone. My failure to speak up about the jury nobbling had let a murderer walk free. I didn't return to work that afternoon, instead I walked all the way home, across London. Even then I couldn't face being alone in the flat or talking to my flatmate when she returned home after work. I went to a local pub and downed several gin and tonics. By the time I emerged, dizzy and sick, it was dark outside. I got back to my flat and there was a large, padded envelope on the hallway floor with my name printed on the front. If I hadn't been drunk I may not have opened the envelope, because it wasn't until later that I

*realised it could have contained a bomb. But I did open it
and I removed stacks of fifty pound notes. I laid them out
on my bed and counted them. Five thousand pounds in
cash. If I was confused before, I was even more so now. I
had no idea what to do. Should I go to the police or tell my
boss? But wasn't that all too late? Besides, Aaron had
warned me I'd end up dead if I breathed a word, and he
knew all about my family so he'd probably harm them too.
Then I thought, what I could do with five grand? My
parents could have a holiday, perhaps Mum's last holiday,
and so could I. But it wasn't just the money, Aaron's threat
was what scared me the most. It wasn't just my life that
was at stake but that of my family's. How could I put them
at risk for my cowardice? I couldn't. Instead I used the
money in dribs and drabs. I told Mum that I'd been given a
bonus at work and I wanted her and Dad to spend a long
weekend in a hotel on the Dorset coast. It was her last holiday. I lost my zeal for journalism, or perhaps I just became
disillusioned knowing that the truth often didn't prevail.
That hunger for chasing a story vanished overnight and
instead I became scared. A colleague got the promotion that
I'd wanted and that was fine by me, because I knew I'd
never make it to the top. Fear and ambition are forces that
work directly against each other.*

I hold the pen aloft for a moment. I hate myself for
accepting that bribe and I know that if Haydn ever found out,
his respect for me would vanish. So morally principled is my
husband, he'd probably file for divorce. Or would he? We all
do stupid things when we're young, it's just that most of us
aren't haunted by the consequences for decades after. I start
writing again.

A little over a year later, Kyle Franklin killed once more.

This time it made all the newspaper headlines because his
victim wasn't a gang member. Leon Johnson was a brilliant man, a doctor with a glittering future ahead of him,
the victim of a random act of violence by an out-of-control
murderer, married for just two years to a school teacher.
There was public outrage. How could the jury have let
Kyle off in the first place? What a travesty of justice. If he'd
been convicted for Jason's murder he wouldn't have been
able to kill Leon. And what an idiot Kyle was to have been
caught twice. My boss asked me to follow the case since I'd
reported on Kyle's first murder trial. But I couldn't. How
could I sit there in court listening to what horrors Kyle
Franklin had done yet again? How could I listen as the
legal teams explained how he destroyed another innocent
life, a doctor who was on course to help thousands over his
lifetime? How could I look into his wife's eyes and know
that I could have prevented the death of her husband? And
how could I sit there knowing that Aaron's eyes would be
on me every single day, reminding me that I should keep
silent about what I knew. I got myself into a terrible state.
I didn't sleep, I drank too much, I missed deadlines at work.
In the end I knew I had to quit before I was fired. The
insomnia hit in earnest then as I weighed up the impossible
dilemma I faced. I could do nothing. I had every hope that
this jury would be more prudent, less open to corruption
and that they would do the right thing and put Kyle
Franklin behind bars for the rest of his life. But what if
Aaron got up to his old tricks again? From police reports
the case wasn't cut and dried. They thought Kyle was
behind Leon's murder but he hadn't confessed and was
pleading not guilty. I had no idea whether the police had
sufficient evidence.
I had to do something, didn't I? I paced my flat for days,
unsure what course of action to take. And then I received a

text message reminding me not to talk, reminding me that my family and I were being watched, that I was complicit. I was sure I was being followed, even when I nipped out to the shops. How could I go to the police with the threats that were being made to me and my family? I tried calling the number that the text message came from but it never connected. I assumed it was from a burner phone. To make things so much worse, Mum was told that she had just a few weeks to live. I barely left the flat except to visit her in the hospice and I only had one grand left from the bribery money.

Eventually I made a decision. I sent an anonymous note to the court clerk saying that I had evidence that there had been jury intimidation in the previous trial and suggested it might happen again. I gave a description of Aaron and explained that he had threatened me. Of course I was careful to leave no fingerprints, nothing that could lead the type-written note back to me. That day I ventured out, the farthest I'd been from home in weeks. I took the train to Brighton, posted the letter there, and took the next train home. As soon as I got home, I packed up my essential belongings into a rucksack, took the train to Gatwick Airport and bought a one-way ticket to Malaga. I chose the destination simply because it was the cheapest place to fly to that evening. I knew no one there and no one knew me. Three days later, my sister sent me a text message to say Mum had died. Her funeral was two weeks later and I didn't attend. How could I? I was terrified that if I turned up, Aaron would find me and follow me and perhaps the whole of our family would end up in a grave next to Mum. I stayed in Malaga, working in bars for cash, drinking too much and sleeping too little, until eventually I got a job with an English speaking newspaper. I only returned to the UK after I fell in love with Haydn, a man who I knew would keep me safe. Dad didn't speak to me for years, not until after Ollie was born, and I don't blame him. I was a truly terrible daughter.

I can't write any more. Now I'm sobbing, my hand sore from writing, my heart broken. I know Amity is right, that I need to face up to what happened back then, but it's so hard. All I'm relieved about is that I can write this down and not have to speak the words aloud.

12

AMITY

I've been listening to Daisy's pitiful sobs and watching her as she wipes the snot off her nose. I installed a hidden camera, a system that no one else knows about. The lens itself is tiny, built into a light bulb, something that no one would ever detect even if they were looking for it, and it works perfectly well even in low light. I've set it up so that it beams onto my phone through an App that I've password protected and I use triple authentification. I would never dream of doing this to my other guests as I have a deep respect for their privacy, but Daisy McKenzie is different. I need to know what she's doing. She's gulping her cries now, like a toddler unable to control herself.

Enough is enough. I leave my suite, stride down the corridor and knock on her door. It takes a while for the door to ease open.

'Good evening, Daisy,' I say brightly, pretending that I haven't noticed her sore eyes and dripping nose. 'I'm just popping in to say goodnight and to say how brave you are.'

She walks back to the bed and sits down.

I pause as I enter the room, then peer at her. 'Oh goodness, you're not alright, are you?' I take a deep breath before sitting on the edge of her bed next to her, pulling her into my arms and clutching her hard. It's not pleasant being this close to her, touching her like this, but I know I have to be single-minded and put aside my aversions.

'You're being so brave, Daisy. It really is difficult confronting our greatest fears but you are doing such a stellar job.' I feel her relax in my arms so I let go and stand up. 'How are you getting on?'

'It's been hard thinking about things in the past that I'd rather forget.'

I nod as my eyes alight on the journal. It's wide open on the bed, the pen lying to one side. I can see that she's written multiple pages and am relieved that she's proving to be such an obedient pupil, following my instructions to the letter. This will give me all the information I really need.

'Why don't you take a hot bath?' I suggest. I remove a small bottle of bath oil from my pocket. It's expensive oil that we sell to our guests, but I brought the smallest size to give to her. 'Use this lovely oil. It's made from pure rose petals from Morocco; I think you'll love it. In a few minutes, I'll send up one of the waitresses with a special calming drink that will help you relax and sleep.'

'Thank you, Amity,' she says, sniffing as she takes the oil from me.

'Have the bath now,' I say and like a compliant child, she gets up from the bed and walks to the bathroom. I slip out of the room when I hear her bath running, and nip down to the kitchen to make her a tea using a special night-time blend, then I hurry back to her room. I knock gently on the door, but there's no answer. Assuming she's in the bath, I use my master key card to slide the door open. I pause for a moment and can hear her sloshing the water around in the bath. Hurrying to the bedside table, I place the mug on a coaster and open up the journal, then I whip my phone out and take photos of every page.

Thank you very much, Daisy, I think to myself.

I slip out of the room and then knock loudly on the door a couple of times. I hear her shout, 'I'm in the bath.'

I open the door. 'It's just me, Daisy. I'm leaving your tea on the side table. Have a good night.' After moving the cup of tea from the bedside table to the side table which is further away from the journal on her bed, I let myself out of the room, allowing the door to slam loudly behind me.

As I stroll back through the spa I'm feeling on top of the world.

'Hello, Liza,' I say, smiling widely at the girlfriend of a Manchester United football player. 'How are you feeling this evening?'

'Yeah, great, thanks. Fabulous massage this afternoon.'

'I'm glad to hear it,' I say. 'Sleep well.'

And then Rosemary passes me.

'Good evening, Amity,' she says with exuberance. 'This place is a dream. Beyond lovely.'

I smile tightly. There's something off about Rosemary. She's certainly not our normal type of guest and I wonder how she can afford to stay here.

As I stroll from the bedroom corridor towards the dining room, I see a broom that's been left in the corner of a corridor. That annoys me. I want our guest service to be faultless. I pick it up and stride to the reception desk.

'Jenny,' I say, through gritted teeth. 'Find out who left this broom in a public place and tell them it's not good enough.' I drop it on the floor next to her.

She winces slightly. Perhaps it was her. 'Anyway, I'm off home for the night. Have a good evening.'

'Thanks, Amity,' she says.

I walk down the stairs to the underground parking garage

and stride towards my white Porsche, a present from Keith. I double-check my phone is in my handbag and then I slip into the car to drive the very short distance home. I'm looking forward to a glass of white wine, a luxurious bubble bath and my evening read, courtesy of Daisy.

IT'S a two-minute drive from the spa to home, a residential street with fortunately very few street lamps. I press the remote control button for our electric gates and to my dismay see all the lights are on in the house, lighting it up like a Christmas tree. It means only one thing: Keith is home. My heart sinks. Tonight of all nights I wanted to be alone, to read, think, strategise. I groan as I press the second remote control that opens the electric garage door. Keith's shiny navy Bentley is parked in his spot.

Damn. I thought he was staying in London until the weekend. Why didn't he let me know he was coming home? I glance at my phone to double-check I didn't miss a message, but no, there's nothing from him. I wonder if Katia knows.

Katia is our housekeeper. Yes, it's a laugh and a half having a housekeeper, except a lot of the time it isn't. I appreciate how she cooks and keeps the house clean and does all of those mundane tasks, such as collecting Keith's dry cleaning and making sure the kids have the right uniform for school and packing up their trunks at the beginning of every term. But there are downsides. For starters there's the lack of privacy. She has a little studio flat that adjoins to the main house, accessible through the utility room, but I never know when Katia's going to be in the kitchen or busying around, supposedly tidying up. I'm a private person and I don't want her nosying through my things. I like my own space which is why it's been so helpful to have my own suite at the spa. The housekeeping staff know that they can only venture into my rooms to clean with my express permission.

Much of the time, when Keith is away, Katia and I keep to a different timetable. She does whatever she needs to do in the house between 8:30 am to noon and then I give her the rest of the day off. She keeps quiet about this arrangement and naturally it suits us both. When Keith or the kids are home, it's full on for Katia and she very much earns her keep.

The door swings open between the garage and the hallway in the house and Keith is standing there holding up a large glass of white wine, a grin on his face. He's a cheerful man, and although no one could ever describe him as handsome – mainly due to his triple chin and ever-increasing girth – he makes me feel special. That counts for a lot.

'Surprise, surprise!' he says as I climb out of the car.

'How come you didn't tell me?' I ask. 'I'd have come home earlier.' That's not strictly true.

'I told Katia and she's made your favourite supper of Dover sole. You haven't eaten, have you?'

'No,' I say truthfully. I was planning on making myself an omelette and the last thing I feel like is a full-blown meal.

I put my arms around his neck and kiss him on the lips. With one hand holding the glass of wine out to the side, he puts the other one around me and squeezes my backside.

'I've missed you, my beautiful wife,' he murmurs.

I follow Keith into the living room where he pours me a glass of wine and then sinks into his favourite black-leather armchair. It is huge and squidgy and very unattractive, but it has all sorts of massage and heating functions and Keith loves it. It looks at odds with our modern, white-leather sofa and chairs, but Keith was never going to compromise on his chair. He let me choose all the other furniture in the house, so I can't object.

'How are things, darling?' he asks.

'Good. Work is going well.'

'And the kids?'

'Kitty has got her grade-five piano exam next week which she's stressing about, and Jaxton... well he's just Jaxton.' Kitty is fourteen, as she is constantly reminding me, while Jaxton has just turned twelve. They attending the same co-ed boarding school about an hour's drive from here, and come home at the weekends. I wasn't sure about it because neither Keith nor I went to private schools let alone a boarding school, but Keith was adamant that they have the best education money can buy. In fact the best of everything. I think the boarding school decision was more to do with the type of people they're meeting at such an establishment, but Keith would never openly admit that. Of course it suits me too; the parents are exactly the type of wealthy clientele I am attracting to The Serenity Spa.

'My boy,' Keith says, puffing his chest out as he always does when he talks about our son.

'He's still mucking around in class, acting the joker, getting into trouble.' I sigh. 'His housemaster called me two days ago.' Kitty is the easy child, while Jaxton arrived into the world screaming and he's been manic ever since.

'I was thrown out of school at fifteen and it didn't do me any harm. The boy's got gumption and chutzpah and that's all you need in life. A chip off the old block he is.'

Keith rolls out that line whenever we talk about Jaxton. The boy can do no wrong and he's always been the child that Keith shows the most interest in. I used to think it was because Kitty isn't his but now I reckon he's just chauvinistic. Keith might be proud of me being a psychologist and having my own business, but no woman could ever really compete with him in his male world. I've given up trying. I know some people wouldn't put up with that but Keith has given me so much: money, freedom, uncomplicated love, and I reckon it's a small price to pay. I'm nothing if not pragmatic.

Perhaps it's the same in most marriages, but Keith and my relationship is definitely easier when the kids are at home. I suppose they're our buffer and give us something to talk about.

'Oh, I nearly forgot,' he says. He bounces out of the chair, surprisingly agile for someone quite so large, and paces over to his jacket that he's flung across the back of the sofa. He delves into a pocket and produces a small box. 'This, my one and only, is for you.'

'Why do I deserve a present?' I ask, opening the box with a grin.

'I'm doing well, you're doing well and life is good. Besides, diamonds are the best investment.'

I flip up the navy-blue lid and inside is a pair of stunning diamond earrings, huge, pear-shaped and sparkling. 'Wow,' I say, slipping one earring out. 'It's not even my birthday.'

'Every day is a birthday with you, my gorgeous wifey. Put them on.'

I model them for Keith, who then leans in and gives me a long and slobbery kiss. When Katia knocks on the door and tells us supper is ready, it's a relief. We walk together to the dining room where Keith likes to eat. It's a lovely room with a wide, glass window looking out onto the seafront – not that it's visible as it's dark now. The walls are painted white throughout the house but I softened the look in here, with duck-egg-blue curtains and a large chandelier made from clear glass and pale-blue glass pendants, imported at great expense from Italy. The table is made from a transparent perspex, so no playing footsie in our dining room, and the chairs are those ghost chairs that have probably had their day, but Keith is still fond of them.

'Smells delicious,' Keith says, as Katia carries in a large

platter of food and places it on the silver-coloured sideboard. She puts the food on our plates and then leaves us to it. As is normal these days, I search for conversation.

'Things are going well at the spa,' I say, chewing a small forkful of well-cooked Dover sole. Keith doesn't like fish so he has fillet steak, very well done – massacred in my opinion. 'I welcomed my first guest into the new sleep clinic this week and she's making good progress.'

'I'm glad you're spending my money wisely. Insomnia is a good investment. Half the world complains about their quality of sleep. Did you follow up with the PR agency I suggested?'

'Yes, and they recommended a few journalists to come and stay at the spa and write reviews. There's one staying at the moment, actually.'

'One of the reasons I like logistics. Don't have to worry about branding and consumer interfacing. You're a pretty face, my darling, and will look fabulous in a photo shoot. Thank heavens I don't have to worry about stuff like that.' He chews noisily on a chunk of beef. 'The cost of fuel is proving a bloody nightmare though, all the prices are shooting through the roof. But Craig is meeting with some chap in China about a new innovation in cold storage solutions which can cut fuel consumption in half. If it does what it promises, there'll be a lovely necklace to match those earrings soon enough.'

I pretend that I'm interested in Keith's business but I'm not. I just can't get excited about global logistics, how widgets are moved from one continent to the next or how fresh produce is stored on a ship. Keith tells me things in passing but I don't take it in. I'm just grateful that he lavishes his cash on me and the kids and that we want for nothing.

After the meal, which ends with sticky toffee pudding for

Keith and a herbal tea for me, I thank Katia as I always do, and get up from the table.

'I've got a bit of work to do before bed,' I say, eager to read the pages that Daisy wrote.

'Oh no you don't, my lovely,' Keith says, grabbing me around the waist as I try to walk past him. 'I've been gone for almost a fortnight and I've missed you. Your work can wait.' He nuzzles into my breasts and I try not to let my annoyance show. 'Let's watch a film,' he suggests.

He grabs my hand and leads me downstairs to the basement movie room. There are eight gigantic chairs lined up in two rows and I sink down into one of the chairs in the centre of the room. I rarely come down here. Keith is the movie buff and he likes to watch films with the kids.

'Any strong feelings on what to watch?' he asks.

'You choose,' I say, although I don't know why I bother because we always end up watching what Keith wants. His house, his movie room, his choice. Not that he'd ever see it that way; in fact I know for sure he'd be shocked that's what I think. He's kind to me and a gift of beautiful jewellery is commonplace. In return, I make his home life as easy as possible.

'It's Oscar-nominated,' he says, as he plonks himself down on the chair next to me with a grunt.

The film is boring and surprisingly violent for an Oscar-nominated film. I wish I'd brought my phone with me so I could surreptitiously read on it, but instead I sit through the rubbish for nearly two hours.

'Beddiebyes,' he says to me when it's finished.

'I just need–'

'Tomorrow is another day,' Keith says, cupping his hands around my face. 'Come on, I want my beautiful wife.'

I let Keith make love to me. He is a good lover, generous and thoughtful, happy to put my needs before his own, even if he doesn't fill me with lust and excitement. I definitely wouldn't have married him if it had been any different; my problem is that Keith is not the person I want to be with. So however hard he tries, my mind is always elsewhere, with someone else. Most of the time I fake an orgasm, just to get it all over and done with quickly, and tonight is no different. I feel sad, not just because I'm dreaming of being in another person's arms, but also because I'm not the sex-loving woman that my husband thinks I am.

As he collapses heavily on top of me, his breath ragged, his heavy body crushing mine, I reach up and wipe the tears away from my eyes. As I always do.

13

The hot bath with the glorious essential oil that Amity gave me relaxes my exhausted body and settles my weary brain. She's right, I do feel a sense of unburdening now I've written everything down. The only problem is, I can't stop thinking about what happened in that second court case while I was hiding away in Spain.

I get out of the bath and drink the herbal tea she left me, which is now cold. I wonder whether I should continue writing down my memories, but I don't have the energy. Instead, I lie in bed and recall that time.

Everything I learned about Leon Johnson's brutal murder was discovered second-hand, but it was easy enough to find out what happened through online reporting and English newspapers. Goodness, I was a mess back then. I was grieving Mum, yet I couldn't return to be with Dad and my sister. I had to pretend I didn't care, when in fact my heart was breaking. At the end of a two week trial, Kyle Franklin was found guilty. The judge subsequently sentenced him to life in prison for the murder of Leon. He then admitted to the murder of Jason, so he'll be incarcerated in a maximum security jail for the rest of his life.

I scoured the news every day to try to work out whether Kyle was sentenced because I tipped off the court clerk or because the prosecution just had a stronger case against him this time around. But there was nothing about jury influencing in the Leon murder trial. After the sentencing I became even more paranoid. What if the jury nobbler blamed Kyle's incarceration on me? What if he tipped up in Spain and knifed me on my way home from work, or he did something terrible to Dad or my sister, Marnie? That fear consumed me for about three months and then to my relief, I found an article about jury intimidation, just a small paragraph tucked away in the middle of *The Times*.

Aaron Sullivan was prosecuted for intimidating a member of the jury in Kyle Franklin's first trial and consequently reverting the course of justice. It turns out that Aaron was Kyle's cousin and he got sent to jail for four years for jury nobbling. The jury spokesman confessed to accepting bribes and he was given time too. To begin with, their convictions gave me an overwhelming relief. The horrors were all over while all the guilty defendants were behind bars. I partied hard and tried to forget that I was meant to be grieving the loss of my mum. And then one evening I spilled a drink down the front of a cute English guy in Marbella who was attending a stag party. We got talking, he asked for my number and I fell in love. Just like that. Haydn and I tried the long-distance romance thing but it didn't work for either of us. I had no choice: it was time for me to go home.

Back in England I didn't feel safe. In fact I became obsessed that one of Aaron's minions might find me and seek revenge. The insomnia began. The only way I could dispel my fears was to understand exactly what was said at both trials. I went to the newspaper library and I applied for and scoured the trial transcripts. That was a big mistake. Sometimes ignorance really is best.

The spokesperson in the first trial admitted he knew that Aaron Sullivan had threatened a journalist, and that journalist knew about the jury nobbling, but fortunately for both of them, the journalist never spoke out. How did he know about me? Did Aaron tell him or did he see Aaron and me together either outside Acton train station or at the courts? With shaking fingers and ragged breath, I studied every news report on Kyle's and Aaron's trials but my name wasn't mentioned anywhere.

A couple of commentators said they thought it very unlikely that a journalist knew about the jury nobbling because any investigative journalist worth their salt would have exposed the crime. But I wasn't a journalist worth my salt; I was a young girl, terrified for my life, grieving the imminent and premature death of my mother from cancer, scared for the rest of the family. Eventually I convinced myself that my name wasn't anywhere in the public domain related to Kyle's trials but that it wouldn't stop Aaron and his mates from coming after me. Except in those first four years they didn't. Aaron was in prison and I slowly came to accept that while he was incarcerated, I might be safe.

That didn't mean the guilt wasn't overwhelming. I had Leon's blood on my hands. If I'd spoken out during Kyle's first trial, he would have been found guilty, and innocent Leon would never have died. And Leon really was innocent, not like Jason the gang member. The papers said Leon was a newly qualified doctor from a middle-class family with patients who adored him. He was married to his childhood sweetheart for only a short time. The poor doctor was just in the wrong place at the wrong time and he didn't deserve to die.

I started working for a retail trade magazine. It wasn't

high-flying or exciting, and since then I've come to accept that I'll never have my dream job; it's far too late for that. Haydn and I got married and I pretended my lack of sleep was due to the excitement of our relationship, compounded by the birth of Millie. But the truth was, Aaron was released just two years after he was convicted, and within a month he gave me his first reminder: a little whisper in my ear when I was standing waiting for a train.

'I'm watching,' he whispered. 'If you say a word, you're dead.' And then he was gone.

Over the years I wondered about Aaron's motivation, since he served his time for jury nobbling and was unlikely to be convicted again. I reckon he just wanted to punish me, to make it known it was my fault he ended up serving time. I think he's just a sadistic, evil man who wants to make sure I never forget that I was responsible for his downfall, and the best way to do that was to keep me constantly on edge, terrified as to what he might do next. Perhaps he's worried that I might confess one day and that would have further implications for him.

If that's what he thinks he's wrong, because I can never tell anyone what I did. If I do, it will mean me going to jail. I am the guilty one here: guilty of accepting Aaron's bribe, for becoming an accessory to the crime and for contempt of court. If Kyle Franklin or Aaron Sullivan ever mention my name and sell me out, then I will be prosecuted. I have lived with that terror for years now. My family needs me; they need my income, my support and my love, and I simply can't not be there for my children.

THE LIGHTS TURN out by themselves and a gentle voice I don't recognise talks me through a relaxation exercise where I'm supposed to concentrate and let go of every part of my body. Surprisingly, considering all the emotions revisiting my fears brought to the surface, I slip quickly into sleep. I only know that because I'm suddenly startled awake. My heart is pumping fast, adrenaline is racing through my body. I sit bolt upright in bed and listen. What was it I heard? But there's no sound and the room is pitch black. I do some deep breathing, sink back onto my soft pillows and eventually drift back to sleep again.

Once more I'm awake but I'm not even in bed. What the hell?

I'm walking and I've just bashed into something. I screech. Where am I?

It takes me a few moments to remember I'm in my room at the spa. What am I doing?

I've never sleepwalked before. I put my hands up to my head which feels like it's going to explode. I whimper as I fumble around and find the curtains, pulling them apart, feeling utter relief when I see the moon lighting up the sea in little silvery patches. I put my hands on the cool glass to calm myself, and look down at the beach.

Something moves, casting a faint shadow over the pebbly beach. Is that a person?

I stare harder. Perhaps it's a shadow from the clouds. But then it moves again and I catch the glimpse of a face, lit up by the moon. The person's profile is familiar and I gasp. I swear it looks just like Aaron.

'No!' I exclaim and step back from the window, letting the heavy, blackout curtains plunge the room back into darkness. This must be my mind playing tricks on me; just all those thoughts of Aaron combined with the insomnia.

I bash my palm against my forehead, slapping myself several times.

'Pull yourself together!' I say aloud, although I do open

the curtains again and have another peek. I can't see anyone now.

I stumble towards the bathroom, glad for the blue light so at least I can see. Grabbing a bathrobe and putting it on, I sit on the toilet and stay there, huddled with my arms around myself for a very long time. At least it's not pitch black in here, *and* I can lock the door, so I feel safe.

I try to be rational. I am safe here at the spa and these crazy feelings only happen at night. After almost nodding off to sleep seated on the toilet, I make my way back to bed and once again drop off into oblivion. When I awake, once more with a thudding heart and an overwhelming sense of doom, I know for sure that something is wrong. Why do I keep waking up like this? Surely this isn't right. I want to get out of this room.

I pull the curtains open to get some light, put the dressing gown on again and walk to the door. I unlock it and step out into the dimly lit corridor where all is silent. I walk briskly towards reception wondering what time it is.

There's a man sitting at the desk and as I stand to one side, I can see he's watching a Netflix film on his laptop.

I clear my throat and he looks up, his eyes wide.

'Sorry to disturb you but I can't sleep.' I sound ridiculous, like a child interrupting her parents during a dinner party. 'I'm Daisy McKenzie, on the insomnia programme and it's pitch dark in my room. On purpose.'

'Do you want me to wake Amity?' he asks, a look of concern flickering over his face. 'She doesn't live on site.'

'No, no, it's fine. I was just wondering if I could stay in the lounge, put my legs up on a sofa, so I'm not lying in the pitch black, unless of course you can switch on the lights in my room?'

'Yes, of course you can stay in the lounge. Would you like

a herbal tea or anything to eat? I can nip down to the kitchen and see if there are any snacks in the fridge.'

'No, I'm fine,' I say, although clearly I'm not, and that is reflected in the young man's face. 'What time is it?'

He glances at his computer. '2:35 am.'

That's crazy. I assumed it would be at least 4 am. I've barely slept.

'I'll get you a blanket,' he says, jumping up and disappearing into a built-in cupboard in the hallway that is so well-concealed you wouldn't know it was there.

I meander into the living room where the curtains are pulled closed and a soft, dim light comes from two table lamps. The receptionist hands me a cuddly, angora blanket in white and I snuggle up on one of the sofas.

This isn't working. I know Amity means well but I can't stay here. My body is utterly exhausted and it feels as if my brain is shutting down. I don't want to think about the past; I don't want to explore the roots of my sleeplessness. All I want is to go home and be with Haydn and the children. No job is worth feeling like this.

I make a decision: I will still write a review. I have enough material to say what a lovely place this is, how impressive Amity is and I can applaud her ambition. It should be enough to appease Garth and I'll reassure Amity that I'll only write good things about the spa, because I assume that's all she cares about. Yes, my decision has been made. After breakfast, I am going home.

14

I wake early and tiptoe out of the bedroom so as not to wake Keith. I don't know why I bother because he sleeps so heavily, snoring loudly, dead to the world. Once again, it's my favourite time of day, and it bodes well, with a clear, pale-blue sky and the sea that looks like a mirror. After drinking hot water with freshly squeezed lemon, I decide to do some yoga and then read Daisy's diary. There'll be plenty of time before Keith gets up.

I lay my yoga mat in front of the vast expanse of glass in the living room. In the summer, I do my practice on the deck, enjoying the cool air on my body, but this morning, it's too cold. After twenty minutes, my body feels limbered up and flexible, my mind calm and focused, ready for whatever the day may bring. I walk briskly back to the kitchen.

Where is my phone? I thought I left it next to the fruit bowl on the island unit, but it's not there. I scour the kitchen and find it underneath Keith's unopened post. He's not a tidy person like me; if I wasn't around, Keith's belongings would be scattered everywhere, bills unpaid, the fridge empty. It's a wonder that he has such a successful business empire, considering how messy he is.

I glance at the phone and see I have a message. Clicking on it, my heart plummets. It was sent at 5 am from our night manager. 'Just to let you know that Daisy McKenzie spent most of the night in the living room on the sofa.'

What the hell! My staff know that they need to call me on the landline at home if there's a problem and that most definitely is a problem. I practice what I preach and won't allow Wi-Fi devices in the bedroom.

I glance at the time. It's nearly 7:15 am and I want to read Daisy's diary before Keith gets up. But this makes me livid. I should have been summoned to the spa and I could have dealt with Daisy in the night. Pacing around the kitchen, I take a few deep breaths, calming myself and trying to be rational. Nothing is too awry. I sit on one of the island stools and open up my photos, and then I hear heavy footsteps ambling down the stairs.

'Morning, doll!' Keith says as he lumbers into the kitchen. 'Sleep well?' Why is he up so early? Keith walks up to me and nuzzles his face into my neck. I switch off the phone and place it face down on the marble counter. 'Fancy a bit more of my loving?' he asks, breathing heavily into my ear.

Keith is wearing some sloppy jogging bottoms and his fat belly hangs over the top of the tight, elasticated waistband. I pull myself away.

'Sorry, but I need to go to work.'

'Oh no you don't. I want to have a leisurely breakfast with my wife and then we can hop back to bed for a bit. I've missed you.'

'That's sweet, Keith, but—'

'No buts.' He pulls me towards him so I slip off the stool. This is exactly what I don't want or need this morning: Keith and his fumbling hands.

'Sorry, love, but I'm really not in the mood.'

Keith steps away because he's not the sort of man to force himself on anyone. That's what I like about my husband. He's strong and resolute but respectful towards me and caring. He groans and turns towards the stove.

'Right, what do you want for breakfast?'

'I think I might pass. I need to get to the spa.'

Keith whips around. 'No, love. I want to spend some time with you. We barely see each other these days. The spa was meant to be a distraction for you, something to keep you busy when I'm away, not to take over your life. You and me are what's important. Our marriage. Work can wait.'

I know I can't object to that. It's Keith who made everything possible. It was his money that allowed me to buy the ancient bungalow down the road and spend millions converting it into luxury spa. It's Keith who has facilitated my life as it is today, and for that I'll be eternally grateful. So as much as I'd like to sit down and read Daisy's diary, as much as I'd like to scuttle over to the spa and start my next round of hypnotherapy on Daisy, it will all have to wait.

Keith puts on an apron with words across the front that says, 'Dad fries up some eggs'.

'When am I seeing the kiddos?' he asks.

'Saturday. They're home early because it's an exeat. No hanging around for sports matches or the like.'

'That's good. We should do something special at the weekend. Take them somewhere, have some fun family time.' Keith's idea of a family day out is likely to be Chessington World of Adventures or some other theme park. For a man who loves his luxury, many of his tastes are really quite simple.

'Whatever you like,' I say, placing a kiss on his cheek. I pour us both a glass of freshly squeezed orange juice and then my mobile phone rings.

'Hello, Amity, it's Jenny. Just wanted to let you know that Daisy McKenzie has asked for her car keys. She wants to leave.'

I bite down on my tongue and swallow my metallic-tasting blood. I know I must stay calm for everyone's sake, not least my own. I take a deep breath and step out into the hallway.

'As you know, Jenny, Daisy is mid-programme, so it would be dangerous for her to leave right now. Could you appease her for half an hour or so, and I'll be over as soon as I can. Under no circumstances are you to give her her car keys. Get her something to drink, a magazine to read or whatever, just make sure she doesn't go anywhere.'

'Understood, Amity,' Jenny says. 'I'll explain that you need to see her before she goes and that you'll be over as soon as you can.'

That's not what I said.

'You stupid, bloody bitch,' I say under my breath, and then I wonder: has Jenny hung up on me? I glance at the phone and only then does the dial tone sound. Shit. I hope she didn't hear that.

I am seething. Absolutely furious. Daisy cannot leave, not now. I'm not nearly finished with her, in fact we're only just getting into the good stuff, the things that are going to be truly impactful.

'Eggs sunny side up,' Keith shouts, breezily. The kitchen extractor is on full blast and hopefully Keith didn't hear what I said to Jenny.

'There's a problem at the spa,' I say as I stride back in. 'I'm so very, very sorry, love, but I'm going to have to go. I'll come home as soon as I can.' I throw my arms around him and grind my hips against him. 'We'll do whatever you want later, okay?'

I feel cheap promising sex as my way out, but right now I

have more important things to deal with, not least containing my fury.

'I'll hold you to that, my gorgeous,' Keith says. 'I was talking to my mate, Pete, the other day and things aren't going too well with his missus. Made me realise how lucky we are to have each other, Amity, to still be in love, to still have the romance and the sex in our relationship. I love you, my gorgeous wifey.' He grins at me and I return the smile. I wonder if he can tell that it's forced.

As I run up our floating glass staircase the anger flows through me. I wonder if my ambitions for Daisy have been too mild. Perhaps making her suffer isn't enough. No, it absolutely isn't. She needs much more than that.

I think Daisy McKenzie needs to die.

15

DAISY

I t is such a relief to have made the decision to go home. My insomnia is something that I need to sort out alone and I'll be able to do that at home surrounded by the people I love. Perhaps we need to increase the security at home, install a few more cameras, put shutters on the windows downstairs. That will make me feel safer.

As soon as it got light, I returned to my room and packed my bag. I don't suppose I'm safe to be driving but once I'm out of here, perhaps I can call Haydn and if he's not too busy, he could hop on the train to come and get me. I'm sure he'll understand. So I walked down the corridor towards reception, pulling my small case behind me. Jenny was there and she smiled at me but when she saw my suitcase a frown wrinkled her forehead.

'I'm afraid I'm going to have to go home,' I said. 'Please can I have my phone and car keys?'

'I'm very sorry, but I don't have them. Amity is the only person with the keys to the car key safe.'

'In which case, could you find Amity for me?'

Jenny glanced at her watch. 'She isn't in yet and I'm not sure–'

'Perhaps you could call her and ask what time she will be in?'

'Of course. Excuse me for a moment.' Jenny disappeared into the back room and closed the door behind her, which was annoying but unsurprising as I'd have liked to listen to her conversation. She was in there quite a while and now she has returned, she is pale, shaken somehow, and I wonder why.

'Amity says she'll be here in half an hour and please can you wait. Can I get you a drink or some magazines to read perhaps whilst you wait?'

That's a surprise. There aren't any magazines or newspapers lying around the spa; in fact there aren't even any novels, only self-help books, the type that tell you that you need to believe in your affirmations, that navel-gazing into your soul will cure all of your problems. I haven't bothered with any of them. I know self-help books are a panacea for many, but they're not for me. I wonder if novels and magazines are considered a distraction somehow, an unwanted link to the outside world.

'A magazine would be lovely,' I say. I walk back to the living room and settle into the sofa I left only an hour or so ago.

Jenny comes back a couple of minutes later with a copy of *Vogue* and yet another herbal tea. I can't drink any more, especially as I hope to be in the car shortly.

'Oh, could I have my phone whilst I wait for the car keys?' I ask.

Jenny shuffles uncomfortably. 'I'm sorry, but I don't have access to the phones either.'

I wonder how that makes her feel, having Amity as the

jailer to this place. She throws me an awkward smile before retreating to her glass desk.

It's nearer forty-five minutes before Amity arrives and I'm getting impatient. I just want to get out of here. She hurries over to me looking surprisingly frazzled. Every day this week her face has looked fresh with that barely there makeup look that probably takes a lot of time to achieve and her clothes neatly pressed, but this morning it's as if she got straight out of bed before racing here, and on the wrong side of it too. In a schadenfreude kind of way it makes me feel better. If perfect Amity isn't always perfect, perhaps there's hope for the rest of us.

'Daisy,' she says, pulling a chair so close to the sofa our knees are almost touching. 'My apologies for not being here earlier. I understand that you had a terrible night and want to go home.'

'Yes,' I say, but she carries on speaking before I can explain more.

'This is totally normal and exactly what I anticipated would happen. I don't like to warn my clients because that's akin to planting a suggestion, but the programme follows a very strict trajectory. As I mentioned before, things get really hard before they get better. It's a bit like an alcoholic who has to sink to rock bottom before starting the road to recovery. The great news is that you've just hit your rock bottom. Today is going to be a wonderfully gentle day. I've booked you in to see Doctor Dhingra first thing for a quick checkup and he will prescribe you some lovely pills that will make you feel better.'

'I don't want to take tranquillisers,' I say, and then think, *actually I don't want to take anything because I intend to get out of here.*

Amity's eyes widen. 'Goodness, we never use such medicines here. I'm talking about natural supplements and over-the-counter painkillers.' Her voice sinks to a whisper. 'We have clients who are detoxing from drugs so we don't even have strong medication on the premises. Please be assured, Daisy, that you've done so incredibly well to get this far and now things are only going to improve.'

'I'm not sure. I hear what you're saying but I really think home is the best place for me.'

'In my professional opinion, that is a very bad idea. It could be dangerous for you to leave midway through the course.' She leans back in her chair and glances up at the ceiling before putting her hands on her knees and again leaning in towards me. 'It's a bit like taking half a course of antibiotics. At best it might provide you with a short term cure but the symptoms will all come back; at worst it could make your suffering much more severe. A couple of years ago, I had a client who left a programme midway through and unfortunately she had to be sectioned the following week.'

I think that's a load of rubbish. I am not vulnerable or ill, just exhausted and sick of the navel-gazing. I suspect that Amity wants me to stay so I'll write a longer article.

'I'll still write the piece,' I say. 'And it'll be positive of course because this place is gorgeous and I can see that the sleep clinic programme would work for most people.'

'Oh, Daisy, I'm not worried about what you write. My single concern is curing you of this debilitating sleeplessness that you've been suffering. Of course a positive article would be great, but I want you to have a genuinely good experience here and so far, I don't think that's been the case. Tell me, if you choose to stay, what would you like to happen today?' She tilts her head to one side waiting for my answer.

I try to focus my exhausted mind. 'I suppose a relaxing

aromatherapy massage, perhaps an Indian head massage and some meditation maybe.'

'You see you've just prescribed yourself the very best medicine. That's exactly what will happen today and the only thing I'll add into that mix will be another hypnotherapy session. What do you say?' She throws me a dazzling smile, her teeth so white, they can only be the product of some treatment. 'And the other thing is, Daisy, I really don't think it's very safe for you to drive, not when you've had so little sleep.'

It's as if Amity knows what I'm thinking because that was my main hesitation for leaving now. At this hour, there's no way that Haydn could come and collect me. He'll be on site somewhere or engrossed in meetings. Perhaps Amity's right. A day of gentle massages sounds glorious and exactly what I need. I can still leave later if I want to.

'Alright,' I say.

'That's marvellous!' Amity claps her hands. 'Now let me go and instruct my team to pamper you today.' She stands up.

'I do have a question,' I say. 'Can members of the public access the beach at night?'

'It's a public right of way, so yes. Why?'

'It's just I thought someone was watching me last night. I saw a face staring up at my window.'

'Did you sleep with your curtains open?'

'No, but when I couldn't sleep I opened them and then I saw someone.'

She sits down again. 'That's a classic symptom of exhaustion. You were likely hallucinating, Daisy. Who was it you thought you saw?'

I'm certainly not going to tell Amity that so I just say, 'A stranger. No one in particular but it freaked me out a bit.'

'No one is going to be wandering along the beachfront and then stopping to stare up at your window. It's your mind playing tricks on you. I'm really sorry that you're going through all of this. It must be so upsetting for you, but let's focus on the end goal. This time next week you'll be sleeping like a baby. Dreamless, refreshing sleep.'

Amity unfurls herself from the chair and smiles as she stands up again. I watch as she walks through the lounge to the hall. That frazzled look has evaporated and she's walking with a ramrod-straight back and a bounce to her step. If only I had her energy and positivity. Of course I don't believe that I'll be sleeping like a baby next week, but any increase in sleep would be wonderful. Four hours perhaps.

THE AROMATHERAPY and Indian head massage are exactly what I was dreaming of. Gentle, sensuous, relaxing, and the young woman who performs both has a wonderful touch, knowing exactly when to exert a little more pressure and when to do smooth, calming, long strokes with her hands. I even drift off while I'm lying on my stomach, floating on a cloud of lavender and geranium. I reassure myself that Amity knows what she's doing and that I should count my blessings to be given all of this free of charge.

At lunchtime, I've been moved to a different table – the best one, right in front of the window with a view onto the sea, and it appears that I'm being given special treatment too, because the waitress pours me a glass of champagne. Some of the other women stare at me, and particularly my glass, with eyes of longing, and it makes me feel a little uncomfortable. I know Amity is trying to impress me, but she really doesn't need to go to such special lengths. Unfortunately the enjoyment lasts for less than five minutes because Rosemary arrives. She has an earnest conversation with the waitress and then scampers to my table, sitting down opposite me.

'You'd have thought they'd put friends together but no. I

had to pretend we didn't know anything about each other. Crazy, isn't it? Anyway, I'm here now so we can have a lovely natter.'

I smile tightly.

'Did you sleep last night?' she asks.

'Not great,' I admit, but I don't tell her that I spent the best part of the night in the lounge and tried to leave this morning.

'I had to resort to my little bottle of brandy. Now, I was wondering when I'm next in London, whether you could show me around your offices. I've never stepped foot in a prestigious office like yours.'

'I hardly think–' but she bats away any objections.

'When you can't sleep, what do you do? I mean, do you get up or read, or as you've got such a good-looking husband, do you get up to nocturnal hanky-panky?' She winks at me and frankly I don't know where to look, let alone what to say.

'I was wondering if I should get myself a toyboy, hook up to Tinder, is it? I'm not really *au fait* with online dating. It's a young person's game. I mean if, heaven forbid, you and Haydn split up, you'd be able pick up a new man in no time.'

My fork hovers midair because how does this woman know the name of my husband, and isn't that the weirdest thing to say? I've been very careful never to share any personal information on friends or family on my Facebook group and my personal account is set to private.

'So what do you suggest, Daisy? Has Amity given you any new tips?'

'Um, no. Just the normal. Meditation and the like.'

'Has she done any therapy on you, you know like CBT or hypnotherapy?'

'A bit.'

'I thought she might. I mean I've never had therapy because I like to avoid all that navel-gazing, but I was wondering whether you and me could have a session together with Amity, since we share the same condition. That's how alcoholics get better, isn't it? Group therapy.'

I can't think of anything worse.

'You don't seem very excited about it.' Rosemary leans towards me, a little piece of spinach is stuck between her large front teeth.

'Um, I'm not sure.'

'You leave it with me. I'll convince Amity it's best to share.'

I can't stand this woman any longer and despite not yet having had dessert, I put my white napkin on the table and stand up. I can't imagine Amity agreeing to the idea and there's no way that I would, but I don't want to burst Rosemary's bubble. Today is meant to be a relaxing day for me.

I leave the dining room and return to the meditation room, where I climb into the pod the farthest from the door. Right now I'm going to do nothing except chill.

16

After leaving Daisy, I'm feeling much calmer and confident that my plans are back on track. It was out of character for me, rushing off without saying goodbye to Keith, not getting changed before coming to the spa and letting panic get to me. I hurry back to my suite and sit on the edge of the bed to call Keith.

'I'm so sorry, darling,' I say, keeping my voice husky. 'I shouldn't have run out on you earlier and I'm deeply regretting not finishing your delicious breakfast.'

'What happened?'

'There was a problem with a guest, the journalist guest who's on the new sleep programme, and it's really important that she writes a good review so I needed to make sure the staff didn't screw up.'

'You and your reviews. You worry too much about them, doll. Which newspaper does she write for?'

'Um, she's freelance,' I lie. 'She's placing the article in *The Times* and in a couple of leading women's magazines.'

'That's amazing. I'm so proud of you, babe. A beautiful

wife, a loving mother and an astute businesswoman. Don't know how I got so lucky.'

That makes me feel really bad. Keith is a good man and I know he adores me. The problem is, I'm not the wife he thinks I am and sometimes that makes me feel guilty. I know he'd rather I was at home when he's there and although he didn't want me to leave this morning, he didn't actually stop me.

'Why don't you come over here and join me for lunch today?' I suggest. I'll make sure the chef whips up one of his favourite dishes.

'Sweet, babe, but I haven't got time. I've got some of those wretched Zoom calls today and need to close on a couple of deals. But I'll make it up to you tonight, alright? Love you, babe,' he says, before ending the call.

As I take a shower and select a clean, white linen dress from my hanger of work clothes I realise how grateful I am for Keith. This certainly wasn't the life I'd planned or imagined for myself, but it could be so very much worse. I know I'm lucky.

I SIT on the armchair next to the window and read through the printouts I made of Daisy's handwritten scrawls using the photographs I took of her journal. My jaw literally drops open as I take in what she's said and how she's described what she did. I'm disgusted that she fled to Spain. She was so weak, so pathetic and an anger and revulsion whips up in my gut, so much so that when I finish reading, I chuck my phone onto the bed. I don't think I've ever felt such hatred and revulsion towards another person.

I stand up and pace, my bare feet sinking into the soft carpet. I'm going to have to ramp things up. I didn't intend for Daisy to die this week but that's what she deserves. A frisson of excitement runs through me. Me, a killer. Have I really got that in me?

How can I pull this off? I'm a wife, a mother, a successful businesswoman, not a murderer or a criminal. I can only do this if I do it without destroying my own life, a life that I've so carefully curated over the past decade. If she does die, how will it look to have a death here at The Serinity Spa? That could kill my business. How can I make this work?

I suppose if Daisy was suicidal and I took steps to intervene and help, then I wouldn't be to blame if Daisy walked into the freezing cold English Channel in the middle of the night and never returned. That wouldn't tarnish the reputation of this place because we're not a hospital, we're not a facility designed to care for people with mental health illnesses. We're a spa and a wellness centre. That must be the answer. A tragic, sad but unpreventable death by suicide. Poor Daisy with her chronic insomnia and mental health struggles. Poor Daisy.

I walk down the corridor to the office. Jenny is on the phone and I wonder if I need to butter her up in case she overheard me call her, *You stupid, bloody bitch*, but Jenny just glances up and nods at me. Perhaps she didn't hear me and if I say something now, I might just be making things worse.

I decide to ignore her and use my key to open up the filing cabinet, where I store my client files. I take notes in line with my psychology training and I'm very conscious of keeping up to date with data protection and confidentiality laws. My notes are generally simpler than some of my psychologist colleagues, not least because I'm working in a non-medical setting. Nevertheless, I'm careful. Despite all the disclaimers our clients sign, I have no desire to be sued for malpractice. I select Daisy's folder and relock the cabinet.

Jenny is off the phone now. 'I'll be in my room if you need me,' I say. 'I've then got another session with Daisy McKenzie who I've persuaded to stay. She's fine now and sorry about earlier. Problems with the kids,' I say, pulling a grimace.

'That's good.' Jenny smiles at me as I leave the room.

'Oh, can you get Doctor Dhingra to give Mrs McKenzie a quick checkup. I want to make sure her blood pressure and the likes are all okay. She had a bit of a wobble last night.'

'Of course,' she says. I don't need to instruct Samesh Dhingra. He knows what my aims are: to solve sleeplessness, and there is no way that he is going to question anything I ask of him. We pay him much too much for that.

Back in my room, I sit at the dressing table and open the file. My notes are scarce, as I tend to just jot down the basics of the problem that the client is presenting with, then I write down the psychological intervention process, the outcome aimed for and any risks that may arise. I go back through what I wrote after my sessions with Daisy. My notes are concise and factual but they're not elaborate enough and require more. I take the bones of what I already wrote for each of my sessions with Daisy, then rewrite on a new sheet of paper and expand upon my concerns for her welfare.

Daisy has mentioned that her life isn't worth living. Tried to explore this. Discussed hallucinations and her increasingly erratic behaviour. We discussed that the insomnia is likely to be an effect of her mental state not the cause. Her self-worth is low and I'm deeply concerned about her; fear she may be having suicidal thoughts.

For yesterday's notes I write similar things, but expand a bit more.

Tried to persuade Daisy to return home as we don't have the resources to care for her with her current mindset. Daisy adamant she is okay. Suggested she get an urgent referral from her GP but she refused. She is determined to stay here as she said our facility was helping her more than any other facility or professionals she's visited in the past. NB: Daisy needs to be monitored 24 hours a day. I will put a rota in place with the staff and put everyone on alert. Will also discuss with Dr Dhingra.

I then tear up the original pages and stuff the remnants into my handbag, alongside the printouts from Daisy's journal. I'll dispose of them at home.

I feel much better now. My options are open and I have covered myself for later, when Daisy disappears into the sea. Now I need to ready myself for my next session with her. It's going to be harder this time, now I know more about what she did. How she accepted that bribe; what effects her actions and lack of action had on the lives of so many people. Sleeplessness is exactly what she deserves and I'm glad that she's suffered for over a decade. Today, I know I'm going to have to draw on every ounce of my acting skills and pretend that I can bear to be in the same room as her. I loathe proverbial expressions, but perhaps this dish really will be best served cold.

'Daisy, how are you feeling now?' I ask as she walks into my treatment room.

'So much better,' she says, settling into the armchair.

'Glad you didn't disappear off home?'

'Absolutely. This morning was wonderful and I felt very spoiled at lunch.'

'I'm glad to hear it.'

'I hope you don't mind me saying but there's another guest who seems overeager to befriend me.'

I frown. I haven't seen any awkward dynamics between guests so far. 'Who's that?'

'Rosemary.'

'Leave it with me and I'll look into it,' I promise. I wonder what Rosemary's story is and what she wants from Daisy. But that will have to wait until later. 'So are you ready for another session of hypnosis?'

'Yes,' she says, but there's hesitation in her voice. 'I don't remember anything from these hypnoses sessions. Is that normal?'

I nod.

Thank goodness. If she did recall what I was saying, my cover would be blown and my world destroyed. But I'm a good hypnotist, and I'm never going to make any suggestions unless I'm sure my client is fully hypnotised. And assuming Daisy relaxes into a deep trance – which she should do considering how chilled she seems right now – today I'm going to ramp things up.

I pull the blinds and turn the lights down low, and can't stop the edges of my lips from twitching into a smile.

Once again, I lead her into a state of relaxation, heavy limbs, down the stairs to her special place.

'When you fall asleep, Daisy, you will see Aaron, the jury nobbler, the man you've been so terrified of all these years. Everything you fear will come true. Your husband will leave you. Your children will come to harm. Your home will burn to ashes. You will be convicted of aiding and abetting a criminal. You will suffer in jail. Your worst nightmares will become reality every time you drift off to sleep.'

She looks so peaceful lying there on my daybed, her eyes flickering under her closed lids. I can't help but relish the power this hypnosis is giving me, the knowledge that this woman's thoughts and beliefs are under my control. And I could go further. I could suggest Daisy walks into the sea at night and carries on walking, so that she never returns. I debate suggesting that now but I'd rather she suffer for a bit longer.

Then there's a knock on the door.

No one is allowed to disturb me during a hypnosis unless there's a dire emergency. My heart thuds. Was I overheard? No, that's not possible. The soundproofing in the spa is of the highest standards – one of my key build briefs. The knock comes again.

'Stay asleep, Daisy. Stay asleep.'

I get up from my chair and pace to the door, opening it a fraction.

'I'm so sorry to disturb you, Amity,' Jenny whispers, 'but there's been a phone call from Kitty's school. The matron says she's sick and that you need to go and collect her.'

My fingers curl around the door frame. 'What's happened?'

'I don't think it's serious. A bug or something,' Jenny says, no doubt noticing how pale I've turned.

I suppose she's right. If it was serious, the school would have called for an ambulance, not requested me to go and collect her.

'Thanks,' I say, dismissing Jenny. But still I have that horrible feeling of dread in the pit of my stomach. I adore Kitty, more than life itself. Yes, I know you shouldn't have a preferred child, and yes, of course I love Jaxton, but Kitty is special.

When Keith first suggested sending the children to boarding school, I was horrified. It was bad enough sending my darling Kitty to day school let alone to board. But Keith was insistent and when he mentioned it to Kitty, she was beside herself with excitement. She seemed to think she was going to some Harry Potteresque school, so off she went bubbling with anticipation while I sobbed my heart out at home. It's been a bit of a bumpy ride; sometimes she loves her school, other times she's homesick. I'd love to pull her out of the establishment but Keith is adamant she must stay. He may be a softie towards me, but he's quite disciplined with the kids. If you start something you must finish it, he says, and I suppose that's a good life lesson.

I turn my attention to Daisy who is still fast asleep. I haven't gone nearly as deep with her as I planned and definitely haven't been able to reinforce the hypnosis messages, but now I have no choice other than to bring her out of the trance. I need to get to Kitty and Daisy is going to have to wait.

She awakens and rubs her eyes.

'I'm afraid I've been called away to an emergency,' I say. 'I'm going to leave you in Jenny's capable hands and she can organise whatever other treatments you would like for the rest of today.'

'Yes, of course,' Daisy says, sleepily. I hurry her out of my room and leave her with Jenny. Then I rush back along the treatment corridor and knock on Doctor Dhingra's door. He's with a patient so I beckon him out to the corridor.

'I want you to give Daisy McKenzie two sleeping pills tonight. Crush them up into her evening drink of almond milk, turmeric and dates.'

He raises an eyebrow at me. 'Please just do it. She needs a decent night's sleep. I'm worried about her but I'll discuss it with you in the morning. My daughter's sick so I need to run.'

FORTY-FIVE MINUTES later I'm at the children's school. It's a monolithic beast of a building, sited at the foot of the South Downs in the middle of nowhere, surrounded by acres of fields and pockets of woodland. There's a type of sentry box with a metal barrier at the entrance; a security guard walks out as I approach. I lower the car window.

'I'm here to collect Kitty Smith, House Two. She's sick.'

He walks back to his little hut, much too slowly in my opinion and I see him picking up a phone. I tap my fingernails on the steering wheel. I wasn't keen on Kitty taking Keith's surname, because Smith is just so very ordinary in comparison to my last name, Augustiago. But when we married and Keith formally adopted Kitty, he was adamant she should share his family name. I conceded and of course when Jaxton was born, it was the right thing to do. When I'm not with Keith, I still call myself Amity Augustiago.

The security barrier lifts up and I speed through. I ignore all of the parking restrictions and dump my Porsche outside the front door to House Two. The school is divided into four houses and the kids are allocated a house based on their personality types. House Two is for the bright, spirited children which sums up my children perfectly. As I get out of the car it strikes me that all I can hear are the birds singing; this place is so quiet you'd never know it was a school. I suppose all the kids are inside concentrating hard. I press the buzzer and keep my finger on it a little too long. Eventually it's opened by a harried woman I don't recognise.

'I'm here to collect Kitty Smith. She's in the sick bay.'

'Yes, Mrs Smith, we were expecting you. Please follow me.'

'Actually it's Ms Augustiago,' I say curtly. I don't normally bother to correct them here at the children's school but this afternoon my nerves are on edge.

I follow the woman along a corridor and up two flights of stairs and along another long corridor. At the end there is a glass door. She swipes the panel on the door frame with a key card and the door clicks open.

We walk past two rooms, each housing two children lying

in single beds. A nurse is taking a child's temperature but she looks up and sees me.

'I'll be with you in a jiffy,' she says with a strong Irish accent.

And then I see Kitty. She's wearing her grey-and-green school uniform and she's sitting on an unmade bed, looking so skinny, fragile and pale, her black curls tied back into a tight ponytail, chewing her fingernails. My heart melts as I stand there for a moment just watching. My beautiful girl who looks just like her father. Leon, the brilliant and adoring man that she never knew.

Today was a glorious day. After Amity had to leave suddenly I had reflexology followed by a guided meditation and Yin Yoga. By supper, I was so languid and tired, I didn't even mind that Rosemary was seated at my table.

'I waited to start until you were here,' she says, as if I would care. 'How was your day, Daisy?'

'Great thanks, and yours?'

'Well, I had a thorough checkup with that Doctor Dhingra. He's very dishy, isn't he?'

'Um,' I say, thinking he is anything but.

'Not in the same league as your husband though.'

That comment wakes me up. 'How do you know Haydn?' I ask.

'Good heavens, I don't know him. If only,' she coos.

'So how do you know what he looks like?'

She reddens. 'I follow you on social media.'

'My personal Facebook and Instagram are set to private.'

'Your husband's isn't. I follow him on Instagram and he posts such lovely photos of you with your children. Then there's that new business of his. Isn't he doing so well? Such lovely decorating.'

I shudder as I imagine Haydn's reaction if he knew he had been described as a decorator, but more importantly, how on earth did I miss the fact Haydn accepts random followers? What is he thinking? Could Aaron have followed me via Haydn? This has been my problem. Haydn has never taken my concerns about security and privacy seriously. I understand why, because I haven't been able to give him a valid reason for my worries. Consequently, he just thinks I'm an overly-anxious person and he humours me, only acting if I force him to. If Rosemary knows about my personal life, anyone could.

'I was a bit disappointed that Amity wasn't here this afternoon. I wanted to ask her about our group therapy. The more I think about it the more hopeful I am that we could both be cured of our insomnia. Wouldn't that be lovely, Daisy?'

I have to grit my teeth because this woman is setting my nerves on edge. She is intrusive and doesn't stop chattering. When the food comes, it is a welcome relief to concentrate on it and I just zone out as Rosemary witters away.

'Daisy?' she says, waving her hand in front of my eyes.

'Sorry.'

'I was just saying that I wondered if I might get chucked out of the spa for it.'

'For what?' I say, hoping that she will be asked to leave.

She lowers her voice to a whisper, leaning so far across the table, her robe dips into her beetroot salad. 'I walked into town this afternoon and went to the library to use the computer. I wrote a little post on *Can't Sleep And Going Crazy* about how lovely this place is.'

'Isn't that against the rules? I thought it was all about relaxing here.'

'I'm a rule breaker, me!' she says, although I find that difficult to believe. She reminds me of my old piano teacher; a staid, middle-aged woman who rapped me on the knuckles when I played a wrong note.

'What did you write?' I ask, my heart sinking, as I think about the implications.

She leans back in her chair, a bright pink slash from the beetroot across the breast of her dressing gown.

'Daisy, Daisy. You've no need to worry, I'm the very epitome of discretion. I just thought it fair that other people get the benefits of this place like you and me. Did you know that I slept four hours last night? Four whole hours. What about you?'

'Not so good,' I say. I beckon the waitress over.

'Please can I have a banana to take back to my room? I'm feeling really tired all of a sudden.'

'Of course.'

A few moments later, I stand up. I hold my breath wondering whether Rosemary will follow suit but she doesn't. 'You sleep well, my lovely,' she says. There is something so saccharine about her tone that it sends a shiver down my spine. I nod and hurry away.

I am approaching my room when a waitress appears, holding a small tray with a mug and a banana.

'This is for you, Daisy. Sleep well.'

'Thank you.'

It is such a relief closing my door, being alone, yet being alone also stirs up the fear and longing to see Ollie and Millie. I take a quick shower and after eating the banana and drinking a delicious almond milk drink, I snuggle down in bed and write a note in my journal to the children telling them how much I'm missing them.

· · ·

THE NEXT THING I KNOW, I'm opening my eyes and there is light coming through the sides of the curtains. How is that possible? I wonder if I'm confused and perhaps it's still yesterday. I peer at my watch and it's 6.05 am. I look again. Did I really just sleep through a whole night? Is that possible?

I sit up in bed and smile. For the first time in years, I think I slept for possibly as long as eight hours. I still feel tired and my legs are heavy but I am filled with hope. There's a dryness in my mouth, but I guess that's to be expected after sleeping so long. This is truly amazing. I think Amity's sleep programme is really beginning to work.

I stand up and stretch, then pad towards the curtains, pulling them open. It is definitely morning and the sun is throwing weak rays over the sea, catching the light on little silvery waves. I glance down at the beach and see three men jogging. The man in the front is portly with balding hair, wearing baggy, black jogging trousers and a white vest. But it's the man wearing a hat at the rear who catches my attention. There's something familiar about him, the way he moves perhaps rather than his physique. I stare, but they're quite far away, and then he turns his head towards the spa and I gasp. He looks just like Aaron.

I take a step back from the window. No, that's not possible.

I look again but they're farther away now and I can only see the backs of their heads. I tug at my hair.

My mind must be playing tricks on me, just as Amity said it would. But I can't tear myself away from the window. I thought I saw him the night before last in the middle of the night and again now. Surely I wouldn't imagine it twice, would I? Perhaps they'll jog back this way and I can get another look.

I perch on the side of the bed and then feel cold, so I wrap myself in a throw from the chair. I wait about fifteen minutes and am about to give up and go to the bathroom when the trio come back into view. Standing just to the side of the curtain, I get a good view of their faces.

I'm wrong. This man is bald with a beard; he's removed his beanie and there's no way he can be Aaron. I feel stupid now, as if I've belittled my progress somehow. Here I am, so pleased for sleeping through the night and now I just confirmed that my mind is playing tricks. How I wish Amity wasn't right.

I take a long shower and then make my way to the dining room. I'm the first guest there and I wish I wasn't. It's only now I'm all alone that I realise how much being around other people keeps me sane. After about five minutes, a waitress appears and pours me a green tea and places a large bowl of homemade granola in front of me. A little while later, Jenny comes over to my table. 'I'm afraid Amity won't be in until later. Her daughter is home from school and she sends her apologies. Amity suggested that you might like a session of floatation therapy.'

'I've always wondered what it feels like,' I say.

'Oh, it's wonderful,' Jenny enthuses. 'It's like lying in a great big bath with a lid and you float on the water. It's meant to deprive you of any sensation, allowing for the ultimate relax. I thoroughly recommend it.'

'Okay, great. I look forward to it.'

'It's best to let your breakfast digest first, so how about I collect you from the lounge in an hour?'

'Thanks, Jenny, that would be great.'

As I'm finishing my breakfast, I think of all the hours that Amity spends here and I wonder how she juggles the spa and her family. Perhaps I can ask her to explain how she manages that tricky balance when I come to write the article.

. . .

THE FLOATATION TANK is a very large, white plastic pod, standing by itself in a room with a tiled floor. There's a walk-in shower to one side.

'You're meant to pull the lid down when you're inside,' Jenny explains. 'And there are two buttons; one which you can call for help and the other is to switch out the lights. Just have a shower and then get in the tub in the nude. Music is piped through for the first ten minutes and again at the end so you know when to get out. Oh, and there's a little float to support your neck. Use the earplugs to keep water out of your ears and there's a spray bottle if you get salt water in your eyes by mistake. Have a wonderful hour.'

I'm just about to step into the shower when there's a knock on the door and Amity pokes her head around. I clutch the towel to cover myself and am surprised to see there's no lock on the door. I suppose it's in case of an emergency.

'Sorry to disturb,' Amity says. 'Just wanted to apologise for not being here first thing. It's really important that you pull the lid right down when you're inside so that the air and water temperature become the same. Also switch the light off, as that will give you the best experience. The temptation is to leave the light on, but your body is in desperate need of maximum sensory deprivation.'

'Okay,' I agree, somewhat warily. I'm not claustrophobic generally but it does seem weird pulling a lid down over one's head.

'Enjoy and I'll see you later.'

And then Amity is gone.

I CLIMB IN GINGERLY. The water is quite warm and only about six inches deep. Weirdly I float immediately and it's difficult to stay in one position long enough to even pull the lid down.

It moves easily enough, and I'm relieved that there's enough height so I can easily sit up should I choose to do so. I use the little float to support my neck and lie back in the warm water. At first it feels really strange but then I realise I could get used to this. It is very relaxing. I move to one side to switch the light button off and now I'm not so comfortable. I switch it back on again. My heart starts racing. What if I can't lift the lid up? I sit up and push at the lid and it lifts easily, cool air seeping into the pod. I feel stupid so I close it again.

I switch the light off and float in the warm water, keeping my eyes firmly closed, although quite why I'm not sure because it's pitch black in here. The music fades out to silence and all I can hear is my own breathing. I don't know how long I lie there but my heart seems to be beating faster and louder. The air is beginning to feel very humid and hot, condensation building on my face. Has it been ten minutes since the music stopped, twenty minutes, three-quarters of an hour? It feels as if I've been in here for a long time.

I move slightly and a lock of my wet hair lands on my face. I try to brush it away but the water is so heavily salted it burns my eyes. And now I am panicked. I can't breathe; it's too hot and I need to see, if only to use the little bottle of water spray to stop the burning in my eyes.

I fumble around and find the big, round rubber button. I press it but nothing happens. I try it again and still nothing. Am I pressing the right one? Could I have got turned around?

I reach to the other side for the button that I think Jenny said was the emergency button and I press my palm on that. There is no noise and again, nothing happens. Now it feels as if the darkness is coming for me from every angle, pushing down on my chest, closing up my windpipe. I have to get out of here. Now.

I push my hands upwards so they touch the rounded surface of the pod's lid and I push. Nothing happens. That can't be right. When I tried it earlier, the lid lifted up easily on sprung hinges. I try again. It feels as if I'm locked in here, stuck in an overwhelmingly humid box in the nude, with a finite amount of air. Am I going to suffocate, boil perhaps?

'Let me out!' I scream but my voice sounds leaden as if it's incapable of permeating through the thick walls of plastic. 'Help! Let me out!'

I'm thrashing around now and the burning salt water has got into my mouth and one of the wax earplugs has dislodged from my ear, the salted water searing my ear canal.

'Please, I need to get out!' I'm sobbing, desperate like a terrified child stuck in a cupboard. My logical brain is telling me I need to calm down, to do slow deep breathing, but the panic is stronger. I must be locked in. Was it on purpose?

And then I remember the episode in the sauna and how I couldn't get out and assumed the worst. I felt like such an idiot afterwards when Jenny showed me how easy it was to open the latch. It must be me, being foolish.

I take a deep breath of hot, salty air and push my hands up against the lid again. Nothing. Perhaps I'm not in the right location. I fumble around so that my back is up against the side where I'm sure I was sitting originally, but how can I be sure? It's pitch black in here. I push upwards once more and still the lid is firmly closed, not giving at all.

What if I've been left in here to die? What if no one comes to get me? How much air is there and how long can I survive? I know I'm being stupid but it's impossible to be rational. My heart feels as if it's going to beat out of my chest and salty tears are running down my already salted face.

I scream.

18

I knew Daisy would struggle in the floatation tank. In truth, most people don't manage to turn the light off during their first session. It's a strange sensation, blissful when you relax and get into it but Daisy is highly strung at the best of times.

I can hear her thrashing around inside the pod, trying so hard to push it open and failing. Her sobs are pitiful and for a moment I actually feel a little sorry for her. I illuminate my watch and see she's been in there for just over half an hour. I wonder if I should let her drown. I'm sure that's possible, even in such a small body of water. It could be rather convenient considering the floatation tank is filled with heavily salted water, just like the sea. But how would I get her body out of the spa and down to the sea without anyone seeing me? That would be nigh impossible to do alone and even if I pulled it off, the pathology reports might show that the saltwater in her lungs and stomach is much more salted than water from the English Channel.

I discount the idea. No, I'll stick to my original plan of hypnotising her so that she walks into the sea and carries on walking, drowning somewhere off the Sussex coast. I release my hold on the lid, step towards the door and switch the light on.

'Daisy,' I say, rushing forward and lifting the lid up. 'Oh my goodness! What happened?'

She's totally naked – not a pretty sight, as she clearly hasn't bothered to look after herself – and she's desperate. Gasping for air, her eyes bright red and streaming from the salt, she slips and slides as she tries to get out of the pod. I grab her white fluffy towel and wrap it around her, holding her arm as she stumbles out of the pod and collapses in a heap on the tiled floor. I crouch down next to her.

'You need to breathe slowly, Daisy. Breathe in and then breathe out. And again. You are totally safe, nothing has happened to you and nothing is going to happen. It's just your mind playing tricks on you once again. Breathe in, two, three and out, two, three. And in two, three and out two, three.' She whimpers and is still finding it hard to catch her breath.

'You need to pull yourself together, Daisy. You are perfectly safe. You're having a panic attack. Now concentrate on your breaths.' I do the slow breathing with her for four or five minutes until her ragged breathing slows down and she calms.

'I'm sorry,' she says bashfully after a while. And so she should be. What a pathetic show that was.

'I want you to take a shower and get dressed in your underwear and robe, and I'm going to get you a hot drink. We're then going to my therapy room where we'll unpick what just happened. Okay?'

She nods. I offer my arm to help her up.

. . .

ABOUT FIFTEEN MINUTES LATER, Daisy is settled in my therapy room. She looks embarrassed and uneasy and so she should. She's slowly sipping the hot herbal tea.

'Sleeplessness plays with your head,' I explain. 'Often you'll perceive a situation to be reality but it's just a figment of your exhausted brain. We're going to do some CBT and hypnotherapy today. I want you to understand that you're not behaving rationally. What did you think was going on in the floatation tank?'

'That I was locked in. That perhaps I would be left there to die.'

I tilt my head to one side and smile. 'This is a luxury wellness clinic, Daisy. How likely would that be?'

'I know it was stupid,' she says glancing away from me. 'I was scared.'

'You have a lot of fear, don't you? But there's nothing to be fearful of. You're in a safe place here. I want you to acknowledge your fear and accept that it's just an emotion, a feeling that will pass. Think of the word emotion. The word itself has motion in it. All feelings are transitory. I want you to sit here alone for a few minutes and truly absorb that. You have nothing to fear. Absolutely nothing.' I look her straight in the eyes and I'm impressed by how eloquently I'm able to lie, because Daisy should be fearful. Very fearful. I stand up. 'I'll be back shortly.'

I walk out of the room and meander slowly down the corridor. I can't decide what my next steps should be. I could ramp up her daytime fearfulness, but perhaps it might be better to quell it so that the fear around sleep becomes even more poignant. Besides, I want Daisy to suffer as much as possible before she dies and I'm on track to achieving that.

'Mum!'

I jump. I forgot Kitty is here and immediately feel guilty.

'Hello, darling!' I put my arms around her skinny shoulders. It was perfectly obvious that there was nothing wrong with Kitty this morning and when I pushed her a little, she admitted that she wasn't ill but homesick. I swept her into a big hug and when she asked if she could stay at home for a day or two, I was hardly going to say no. Keith thought Kitty should have gone back to school today but then he's always harder on her than he is on Jaxton. I made up a little white lie saying that Kitty had awful period pains, knowing Keith would never question that. Besides he had to hurry off to some meeting this morning. When Kitty asked if she could have a massage in the spa, of course I was going to indulge her. She's a good girl who always gets excellent school reports, and it's not easy being fourteen and living in a boarding school.

'Did you enjoy your massage?' I ask, as we walk side by side. She's grown so much recently; I expect she'll be taller than me in a year or so. Her dad was tall, much taller than Keith.

'It was Gucci. I'm so chilled now. But what was the scream, Mum? It sounded awful. Was it a real person?'

I have to hide my snigger because of course it was a real person, but I fib to my beautiful daughter. 'It was part of a therapy session, seeing how someone reacts to a stressful situation.'

'Oh,' she says. 'You're not going to do any of your weird therapy on me, are you?'

'You're safe. It's bad practice to work on close friends and family. I could hardly be objective around you, my gorgeous girl, could I?'

I kiss her cheek and she wriggles away from me. The love I have for Kitty is so fierce, I would do anything to protect her. Literally anything. I know that I'm sometimes overprotective, but she has no idea what a difficult start she had in life, how broken I was for those final months of my pregnancy. Kitty knows Keith isn't her real father but nevertheless, he is her daddy, the only male role model in her life and for better or worse, she adores him. All we told her is that her real daddy died before she was born and that he watches her from heaven. Sometimes she asks about him and I fob her off with little mundanities, made up mostly. I don't want her to know that her father was stabbed to death in a horrible, random attack. No child should grow up with the fear that life can be taken away in an instant. I will tell her the truth one day, but only when she's mature enough to handle it.

'I'll walk you home,' I say. It will take at least half an hour to walk there and back but that's alright. It will be good to keep Daisy waiting. 'Katia is at home and she can keep an eye on you. Do a bit of homework and not too much Netflix, okay?' Kitty nods.

AFTER DROPPING Kitty off at home, I amble slowly along the seashore back to the spa. I think back to when I met Keith, how very fortuitous it all was. I had completed my psychology training and spent a year working for a large practice, but I wanted to be independent and have my own practice. I was looking for premises, just a room or two, a place that I could call my own. I specialised in helping people leave abusive relationships and it was something I felt very strongly about; still do in fact. That's what happens when you're the only child of narcissistic, abusive parents. Fortunately I knew all the signs to look out for and have never been in an abusive relationship myself, except the parental one of course. Then, I was in love, happy and filled with confidence for the future.

I remember a skinny, insignificant estate agent was showing me around an office block in Hammersmith, West London. He was trying to persuade me to take a three-room suite but I was adamant I only needed the smaller two-room office. As we were having a heated discussion in the corridor we came face to face with three men, two of whom were wearing ill-fitting shiny suits, the other was dressed in designer jeans and a jacket. The estate agent, whose name I've forgotten, turned rather red in the face and was embarrassingly smarmy to the tallest and more casually dressed of the three men. It was 'yes sir' this and 'yes sir' that.

When we walked into the lift he whispered, 'He's the owner of the building. He has a vast portfolio of commercial properties and they say he's getting into logistics too. My boss told me if I can get him to agree to us representing him for more properties, I'll get a promotion.' I remember those words but didn't really pay much attention. I was already imagining how I'd decorate my rooms and what my marketing strategy would be to get new clients.

I signed the lease and moved in. It was a few weeks later when building works started. I was trying to have a calming dialogue with a client when the pneumatic drill fired up and it became impossible to talk. This was not how I was going to grow my client list. I apologised and we tried to carry on, but the next day the noise was untenable. I stormed downstairs to confront the concierge.

'These building works are ruining my business!' I exclaimed, running my hands through my hair. 'I took this lease to grow my practice not decimate it.'

'Excuse me, but you are?'

A man stepped forward, wedging himself between me and the concierge.

'More to the point who are you and why are you interrupting my conversation?'

The concierge flinched and it was only then that I vaguely recognised the man. 'My name is Keith Smith and I'm the owner and developer of this property, in other words, I'm your landlord. What's the problem then, love?' He spoke – and still does – with a south London accent, never fully articulating the vowels at the end of words.

'The incessant noise. When I signed the lease I wasn't told there was going to be building works on the other side of my wall. I'm a psychologist and I simply can't work under these conditions.'

'Mmm,' he said, stroking his chin. 'I can see what a nightmare this must be for you, but the works are going to be going on for a few weeks. Didn't that slithery eel of an estate agent tell you?' He doesn't give me time to answer the question. 'I can offer you either a reduction in rent or I can loan you some temporary accommodation in my premier office block off Portland Place. That might be quite convenient for you being so near Harley Street and although I say it myself, it's a better address than this one.' He chuckled and I couldn't help but smile. 'Why don't you go and have a look at it and decide for yourself?' He produced a business card. 'Ask for Suzy. She's my secretary and I'll give her the heads up.'

'Thank you,' I said, surprised and relieved I might have a solution. I hoped my clients wouldn't mind travelling to Portland Place and he was right, it certainly was a better address for me.

The next morning I visited the 'premier' office block and Keith was true to his word. The entrance hall was clad in marble, the door handles were gold and Suzy turned out to be a middle-aged uber-efficient assistant who oversaw every detail of getting me settled in a plush new office twice the size of the rooms in Hammersmith.

Over the next week, I ran into Keith most days. He was always charming, enquiring if I was settled, asking how my business was going and whether my clients liked visiting here. As his politeness and his smart dress sense were at odds with his accent, I assumed he was a poor boy made good. One morning he asked me if I would join him for a coffee at Starbucks. It seemed rude to decline, especially as he had been so helpful. Keith made me roar with laughter over my latte. He was and still is hilarious, when he's not too stressed out over a business deal. He confirmed that he was brought up by his single mother on a Peckham council estate and his teacher told him he'd either become a millionaire or end up in jail. He made his first million by the age of twenty-five.

'I'm going to have to get back otherwise I'll be late for my next client,' I said.

'Will you have dinner with me, Amity?'

I was surprised. We had a laugh but I didn't find Keith in the slightest bit attractive and I didn't get the sense that he was flirting with me. 'I'm sorry, but I'm engaged to be married,' I said, glancing at my left hand where the small diamond sparkled.

Keith's eyes followed mine. 'Was rather hoping that ring was a family heirloom,' he said wistfully. 'Not surprised you're taken. You're a beautiful and intelligent woman.'

I wondered whether Keith might try something on anyway, but he never did. He was always respectful and charming and when it was time for me to move back to the original building, he insisted I stay at the Portland Place office for a very low rent. It was a few days after I signed the new lease that I was hurrying through the lobby, filled with utter excitement, and I tripped slightly. I was fine but the contents of my handbag went flying across the marble floor. To my embarrassment, Keith walked in at just the wrong moment. He bent down and saw my pregnancy stick. My positive pregnancy stick, and the reason I was in such a hurry to return home to tell Leon.

'Is that what I think it is?' he asked. I blushed scarlet.

'Yes.'

'That is truly wonderful news, Amity. I'm delighted for

you. Perhaps you and your fiancé could join me and my girl-friend for dinner one evening?'

'Thanks,' I said, more focused on getting out of the office quickly.

The next day there was a bouquet of flowers outside my office door with a note of congratulations from Keith and the office team. How ironic that Keith was the first person to know about my pregnancy. How ironic that he is now Kitty's father.

19

DAISY

I feel like an idiot. I totally overreacted in the floatation tank, and Amity is right, my nerves are so highly strung due to lack of sleep, I'm unable to react in a rational manner, with panic taking hold. I must have become disorientated in the dark. She keeps me waiting in her office for a long time. I get up and pace the room.

There are just a couple of ornaments on the shelves – a large seashell I assume from somewhere exotic and a painted pot in pale yellow housing a small houseplant. There's Amity's desk and a filing cabinet next to it, both made from the same pale wood. On the wall opposite the main door there's another, and I wonder where it leads. I stand in front of it for a moment and then place my hand on the door handle which opens easily. I ease the door open just a couple of inches and see it's a bedroom, larger than mine but decorated in a similar manner. Deciding not to snoop, I close the door again, walk to the window and look out at the beach.

Amity is there walking along a path, her arm around a mixed-race girl who I assume must be her daughter. They look at each other and laugh and it feels like a spear in the ribs for me, reminding me how much I miss my own children. I only have two days until I can see them again but it feels like a lifetime. I need to hear their voices, find out what they've been doing at school this week and hold them in my arms. Let's hope when I return home I'll feel more present, more able to be a better mother. If I continue to sleep like last night then my life could be truly transformed and all of this will have been worth it.

After twenty minutes, I wonder if Amity has forgotten about me or whether an emergency has come up. I leave her room and walk to the reception desk.

'Just wondering if I should carry on waiting for Amity. She's been gone quite a while.'

'Oh,' Jenny says, frowning. 'Let me give her a call.' Once again she slips into the back office, closing the door so I can't overhear. She's not long this time.

'Amity apologises. She's on her way back and will be with you in five minutes. Would you like a drink whilst you wait?'

'No, I'm fine thanks.'

TEN MINUTES later and Amity strides back in. 'I'm sorry about that. I was a little longer than anticipated.'

'No problem,' I say. 'I'm sorry I overreacted earlier. You were right. I just saw you with your daughter. She's a beautiful girl.'

Amity freezes and a strange expression passes over her face but as quickly as it arrived it's gone and she's back to normal. I wonder if I put my foot in it somehow. Perhaps the girl isn't Amity's daughter.

I quickly change the subject. 'I was wondering when it would be convenient for me to interview you. I'd love to find out more about your work, the research you've done and your successes. It will be great to include that in my article.'

'We need to finish the programme first and then you can ask anything you like. Now we need to focus on you and I'd like to hypnotise you again, as we came out of the session yesterday much too early.'

Something has changed in Amity. Perhaps it's the way she's looking at me, but the smiles have gone and that warm, easy manner has transformed into something brittle. Whereas before she made me feel comfortable, now it's as if she has something else on her mind, as if I'm no longer her centre of attention. I can't put my finger on it but I have an uneasy feeling. Is it because I said I wanted to interview her or has something happened at home? It briefly crosses my mind, who is this woman? Does she really know what she's doing? I think back to how I used to be, always doing my research, an eager, rigorous journalist, yet I did absolutely no research before coming here. Of course I'd heard of Amity, reading about her in other press, but I don't know what qualifications she really has, whether she is a good therapist, whether her clients have had positive results. How I have let things slip over the years.

'Daisy,' Amity interrupts my thoughts. 'I asked if you could get onto the daybed please. We need to start the hypnosis.'

I'm not sure that I want to. I have a gut feeling that something is wrong, that it's a bad idea to allow myself to be hypnotised. Perhaps I need to make a conscious effort to resist it. Slowly, I move to the daybed and climb on it, and as normal, Amity puts the blanket over me. But today I reach my hand into the pocket of my bathrobe and take out my room key card. I press the sharp edge to the palm of my hand in the hope that I can focus on the uncomfortable sensation and not fall under Amity's spell.

Amity follows her normal routine, speaking in a slow, languid, deep tone, taking me down the steps to my special place. But I'm focusing on the sharp edge of the key card, jabbing into the palm of my hand, thinking about Millie and wondering what she's doing at school today. But it's so hard to ignore Amity's words and how her voice pulls me down, relaxes my limbs, makes me feel heavy and tired. My mind wanders off for a while but then I catch something she says. 'Stay awake!'

What? Surely I misheard her? My heart is thumping hard now. I try to still myself but now I can hear Amity's words.

'You will stay awake.'

I try to open my eyes but they stay firmly closed. No! I need to get out of this trance, now.

'Daisy?' Amity says. 'Put your right index finger on your nose.'

I do as I'm told. 'I'm bringing you out of the trance now. One. Two. Three.'

My eyes spring wide open. What the hell happened? Did she tell me to stay awake or did I just catch a sentence that makes no sense amongst paragraphs of genuine script?

'Is everything alright, Daisy?'

'Um, I'm sorry, but I'm feeling a bit hyperactive this morning.'

'What do you remember from the hypnosis?'

'Nothing,' I lie. 'Just the relaxing tone of your voice.' I glance at my watch and am shocked to see that half an hour has passed when I thought I was only on the daybed for five minutes or so. Did I imagine what she said? I swing my legs off the bed.

'I think I could do with some fresh air,' I say. 'I'd like to end the session now.'

Her eyes widen and there is a hardening around her mouth, a scowl even, but then it's quickly swept away. 'Of course. I want this therapy to be client led. We can come back to it this afternoon. Why don't you go for a swim or a jog along the beach, expend some physical energy?'

Only when I'm in the corridor do I take my hand out of my pocket. There is a deep-red indentation where I held the key card and I rub it gently to ease the soreness. I want to find out more about Amity, but it's not easy with the absence of phones and computers. I need to find out about her, not just for myself but for the wellbeing of all the guests here.

As I'm walking through the entrance hall I'm surprised to see Flo. She's wearing a long, camel-coloured coat and trainers with big, white platform heels. A large, brown handbag is dangling from her arm and she's wheeling a suitcase through the main door. I thought she'd already left. I pause for a moment as she exits through the glass door and then I glance around. There's no one at the glass reception desk so I dash after Flo.

'Are you leaving?' I ask.

She spins around. 'Yeah, back to the real world.'

'I thought you'd already gone as you weren't at any meals. I had to put up with Rosemary instead. Sorry,' I say hurriedly, feeling mean.

'Oh poor you. The powers that be wanted me to eat in my room. Probably just as well as I was green with jealousy seeing all the food you got given. Besides, I wasn't feeling too great but I'm better now.'

I walk very close to Flo who frowns when I step into her personal space.

'I know it's not allowed,' I say in a whisper, 'but could I quickly check something on your phone?'

Flo glances back at the entrance to the spa and then giggles. 'It's ridiculous, isn't it? It's like we've resorted to being naughty school girls, breaking the rules.'

'You're right. I understand why they do it, but it's still a bit draconian. Rosemary told me she nipped into town yesterday afternoon and went to the library to post something on Facebook.'

Flo frowns at me. 'I don't think she did. I'm pretty sure she was in the spa all afternoon. She had a massage right after mine and then she was in the meditation room reading a Mills and Boon book. I mean, I might have got that wrong, but she was definitely there some of the time.'

That's weird but I can't think about Rosemary right now, Amity is more important. Flo digs into her large handbag and removes her mobile phone which is a large iPhone in a pink mock-crock case. She unlocks it and hands it to me furtively, using her raincoat as a shield. 'Do you want to make a call or check something online?'

'Check something online if that's okay?'

'Sure. I've got to get my car so I'll do it slowly and give you a bit of time.' She winks at me and trots off around the side of the building. Meanwhile I walk in the opposite direction and find a spot in the shadows next to the wheelie bins. I type *Amity Augustiago* into Google.

Details of the spa come up from various articles, mostly copies of the press release that Garth gave me. I revise the search so that the date search criteria is before the opening of the spa, yet her name is nowhere. That's really odd. If Amity was a practising psychologist before the spa opened then surely she would show up somewhere.

I click onto the British Psychological Society website and search the members database. I'm relieved to see her name but there is no address or website listed. That's strange. Surely if she was a practising clinician there would be more details in the public domain?

I look again, just using the words *Amity*, *Psychologist* and *UK* because perhaps Augustiago is her married name and possibly she's been using her maiden name for her professional practice. There is no one who matches her description.

I'm just pondering what to do next when there's the purr of an engine. Flo is driving a silver Mazda convertible and hovering by the big exit gates. I palm her phone and walk towards her. When she lowers the window, I lean in and try as surreptitiously as possible to pass it back to her.

'Thank you so much, Flo. I hope everything is alright at home regarding the burglary and that you have a wonderful wedding.'

'Good luck with the sleep,' she says, throwing me a wink. 'Oh and good luck with Rosemary!' She laughs, raises the window, then drives nearer to the gates which slide open, and off she goes.

I feel strangely bereft, as if she's the lucky one who got away and I'm left behind. That's a ridiculous feeling of course, because I'm meant to be here to relax if not to enjoy myself. I then realise that I didn't get the chance to delete my browsing history, but I don't suppose it matters if Flo sees I was researching Amity. I just wish I did some research before I came here. I've let my journalism skills slip abysmally and that has to stop.

I look up at the glass building and for the first time notice two discrete security cameras. How many more of those are around the place? I have two choices right now. Either I get the hell out of here or I investigate. The safer option would be to run but this isn't just about me. What if Amity *is* a charlatan and what if she's making all her clients dependent upon her?

I stride back inside with a sense of purpose now. I'm determined to find out the truth about Amity. Hopefully she has nothing to hide; hopefully her methods are orthodox but either way, I will find out.

D aisy mentioning Kitty has infuriated me. How dare she! If she'd been a better person and spoke up when she should have done, Kitty would have her real father. Kyle wouldn't have been free to kill again and Leon, Kitty and I would be living a very different life. Sometimes I wonder about it.

When Leon died, he was still married to Debra, although their relationship was so broken it was in name only. They had been together since high school and Leon said they married because it was expected of them; certainly it was what Debra expected. In his heart of hearts, Leon knew it was the wrong thing to do. And then, after just a year of marriage he met me. He called time on his marriage and instigated divorce proceedings, but after he died, Debra airbrushed that fact out of their shared history. Leon was going to spend the rest of his life with me. The ring on my left finger was a promise ring as we couldn't marry until his divorce came through, but Leon was so excited about the birth of our child and he promised me we would be together by then. I doubt we would have lived in the kind of luxury I experience with

Keith; home probably would have been a very nice semi-detached house in south London, where Kitty would be attending a local day school. It's hard to imagine that Jaxton wouldn't have been born, and that I might have had other children, or maybe Kitty would have been an only child. I might have been too busy continuing my practice to have more children. Leon and I talked about that, how I wanted to carry on working as well as having children. He was supportive, Keith less so. When I was in the depths of my grief having just given birth to Kitty, I was in no fit state to carry on working. My clients all drifted away and I was left with nothing. As I got stronger and happiness returned to my life – a dulled-down version but a form of happiness nevertheless – my thoughts turned back to my career.

'Come on, doll, a mother's place is at home with her little ones,' Keith said. 'It's not like we need the money. Go back to work when they've grown up.'

I didn't have the energy to fight Keith but as the kids got older, I became restless. Keith travels a lot for business and I wanted some new challenges. I oversaw the build of our home but he didn't want me to be part of his business. A few years ago he shifted the focus away from commercial property towards global logistics, something that holds no interest for me.

About two years ago, when we (or at least Keith) decided that both Kitty and Jaxton were going to boarding school, I discovered that the small bungalow on the massive plot just a few doors down was going up for auction. I suggested Keith buy it and I would turn it into an innovative wellness centre. He wasn't keen to begin with but my nagging wore him down. And then Keith got the bit between his teeth and before I knew it, he'd acquired the site at a very low cost and I was in meetings with architects and builders and together we planned The Serinity Spa. Being out of psychology practice for so many years, I had to update my knowledge and skills. That was onerous and my supervisor didn't go easy on me, but when I'm determined to do something, I always achieve it. I was put back on the register of practitioners seven months ago, ready for the opening. Ready for my ultimate challenge.

I want to see true fear in Daisy's eyes. Fear like Leon must have felt when he knew that the serrated-edged knife was going to kill him. I need to up the ante and plant more ideas into Daisy's head. The thing with hypnosis is that it only works if the person is already susceptible to certain thoughts. Daisy isn't suicidal but she is terrified of Aaron. I need to use that to my advantage.

As I walk past the reception desk, Rosemary accosts me.

'Amity, I know you don't have any space on your sleep programme but me and Daisy suffer from the same affliction and I was wondering whether it might be beneficial for us if we had a joint session. I mean, I'm no expert, but addictions are treated in groups, aren't they, and I was thinking that me and Daisy could be partners, be accountable to each other, make sure we keep up the good sleep habits. What do you think?'

What I think is that this woman has serious cheek and that looks can be very deceptive, because I assumed she was some mouse-like middle-aged loser. But as I pause for a moment longer, I wonder whether this might just be a brilliant idea. After all Daisy has already said that Rosemary was being over-friendly. Perhaps I can use this to my advantage.

'Leave it with me, Rosemary,' I say. 'I just need to think through the logistics but you might have a point.'

Rosemary sticks her chest out as if I just gave her a gold star.

'Remind me what your schedule is for later this afternoon.'

'I've got nothing until reflexology at 4:30 pm.'

'Good, I'll see if I can schedule something in. One of the team will notify you.'

'Wonderful!' she says, clapping her hands together as she hurries away.

Oh, Rosemary, you could just be my greatest gift!

Daisy's next session with me is straight after lunch and this time I'm not letting her go.

'We need to unravel your deepest fears, Daisy. I assume it's the jury nobbler that you're the most scared of.'

Daisy looks at me somewhat startled and I glance down at my notes. I haven't made a terrible mistake, have I? She told me this herself, didn't she, it's not just what I read in her journal? 'You told me about him two days ago,' I say quickly.

I hold her gaze because she must believe me, and after a few seconds her shoulders relax. I'm sure she doesn't recall what she has or hasn't told me.

'What was his name?'

'Aaron,' she says quietly. 'How long have you been doing sleep therapy?'

'Sorry?' I say, thrown off course by her question and the non sequitur.

'I was wondering how long you've been helping people with sleep problems.'

I sigh and cross my legs. 'Daisy, you're trying to deflect from an issue that makes you uncomfortable. This session is about you, not me. I already told you that I will answer any questions you have about the programme at the end of the week.' She throws me a strange look so I soften my tone of voice. 'I just want to help you, Daisy. We're here to focus on you.' I glance down at my notebook as if I'm trying to remember Aaron's name. 'Now tell me, what does this Aaron look like?'

Daisy shivers. 'Dark hair, skinny, about five feet ten I guess. Deep-set eyes.'

'Quite ordinary looking, then.'

'I guess.' But her body language suggests otherwise.

'What's the worst that he could do to you?'

'Kill me. Harm my family.'

I pause for a moment. 'That's a very dramatic answer. How realistic do you think it is?'

She shrugs her shoulders. 'He's threatened me in the past.'

'In the past. And no doubt you told the police and they told you there's nothing to worry about?' Obviously she hasn't told the police because that would implicate her, but I'm not going to let on that I know. 'When was the last time you had direct contact with Aaron?'

There's a long silence and I lean closer to encourage her to talk.

'A few years ago.'

'That's my point, Daisy. How realistic is it that he's going to be out to get you after all of this time? It's not like you did anything to aggravate him.'

'That's not true,' Daisy says, tears springing to her eyes. 'It was my evidence that sent him to jail. If I hadn't sent an anonymous note to the clerk of the court, he might have got away with it and Kyle might have gone free once again. It was my fault that Aaron was caught.'

'Oh,' I say, feigning surprise. 'But how long ago was that?'

'Thirteen years.'

'Is it really likely that Aaron would pop up now after all of this time?'

Daisy shrugs.

'It seems as if you're spending a lot of energy focusing on

the past and worrying about the future as opposed to enjoying the moment. Would that be a fair assessment?'

'I suppose so.'

'I'd like to try something a little different. I would like to do some group therapy with Rosemary.'

Daisy almost jumps out of her chair. 'No, I don't want to do that.'

I lean back. 'You see, this is exactly your problem. You need to learn how not to overreact to something that makes you feel uneasy. We will not share anything confidential. This will be similar to an AA meeting where you share only what you want to share, but Rosemary could be good for you. I don't know why you've taken against her but it will be healing for you to explore these feelings of discomfort. Going forward you and Rosemary can be sleep buddies, checking in with each other, making sure that you're maintaining sleep hygiene and sharing your experiences. Remember, Daisy, we don't have to like someone to share with them.'

'I'm not sure–'

I cut her off because I don't want to lose Daisy now we're back on some sort of equilibrium.

'Give it a go. Let's have a safe word and if you're really not coping and want to stop the therapy then you can say the safe word and we'll stop immediately. What would you like the word to be?'

She shrugs her shoulders again.

I think about the forms that Daisy filled in and how she underlined broccoli as being her least favourite food. It seems appropriate to use it.

'How about broccoli?' I say, trying not to snigger as I imagine how impossible it would be to seamlessly incorporate the word into a conversation. She nods and I try not to chuckle aloud.

There's a knock at my door and Rosemary pokes her head around.

'Perfect timing,' I say, getting up and dragging a chair from the other side of the room and positioning it right next to Daisy. 'Come in and make yourself comfortable,' I instruct Rosemary. The older woman looks utterly thrilled to be here and I wonder why. Daisy's face is like thunder and she doesn't even acknowledge Rosemary.

'Rosemary, I understand you also suffer from sleeplessness so I thought it might be a good idea for you both to share your experiences. It can be wonderfully cathartic to know that you're not alone with your condition and although what you're doing with your Facebook group is great, Daisy, there's no substitute for face-to-face support. I'd like you to be there for each other and this in itself can be a great way to boost self-esteem and confidence. If it works for you, then you might continue being buddies after you leave here.'

Rosemary claps her hands together. 'That's a wonderful idea, Amity. Isn't it, Daisy?' She elbows Daisy who looks anything but chuffed.

'Rosemary, as you're so enthusiastic, perhaps you could go first. Tell us how your sleeplessness started and why you think it's not improving.'

'As I told Daisy, it began after I was jilted at the altar. These days I feel such loneliness at night and I feel that Frank made such a terrible mistake. I start thinking about him and then I can't stop. You know, what his life is like now, how his wife has let her looks go, that his grandson is about to start nursery school. I lie there all night wondering.'

'How long ago were you jilted?' Daisy asks with a hint of mockery to her voice, which I don't like.

'It was 7th September 1985.'

I try to stop the surprise showing on my face. This woman

is still being eaten up by something that happened thirty-seven years ago.

'It's a very long time to be grieving,' I say.

'Sometimes these things last a lifetime.' As Rosemary crosses her arms across her chest, I see real sadness in her face.

'Daisy, we've talked about the root of your sleeplessness and I know it's something you're not willing to talk about but perhaps you could share the emotion that it brings up.'

I see Rosemary's eyes light up when I hint that Daisy has a secret. These women are so easy to read.

'Fear,' she says quietly.

'And what would you say to Rosemary, knowing that she lies there at night thinking about something that happened a long time ago?'

She shrugs. 'I'm not the therapist here.'

I ignore the sarcasm. 'How would you feel, Rosemary, knowing that you could contact Daisy in the night if you're struggling to sleep once you're back at home?'

'It would be lovely. But I wouldn't want to disturb you or your lovely husband when you're together at your house.' Rosemary swivels to look at Daisy who is still refusing to meet her eye.

'There's a strange dynamic between you two,' I say, leaning back in my chair. 'Rosemary, you seem very eager to get Daisy's approval whereas you, Daisy, appear not to want anything to do with Rosemary. So often we skirt around these uncomfortable feelings but today I'd like to explore them. "What is it about Daisy that you admire so much, Rosemary?'

'Oh, she's truly lovely. Such a wonderful person with her blog and Facebook page and such a perfect little family. Always prepared to interact and share her wisdom. Obviously now I've met you I can see that you're also a guru-type person, but Daisy, she's such an inspiration to me. Her wise words inspire me every day.'

I have to admit I didn't expect this. I'm going to have to show Rosemary that there's nothing special about Daisy; she's just a cowardly woman who deserves to suffer the consequences of the terrible judgements she made in the past.

'And, Daisy, what do you admire about Rosemary?'

'I don't know her,' she says curtly.

'There's obviously something that's troubling you, Daisy.'

She considers the question for a moment and then lets out a sigh. 'To be honest, I don't know why Rosemary is here. It's like she's followed me here to The Serinity Spa and now she's trying to inveigle her way into my life, letting slip that she knows all about my husband and children. It's creepy, like I'm being stalked.'

Rosemary lets out a gasp and her hand rushes to cover her mouth.

'No!' she exclaims, an expression of dismay on her face. 'I'm not a stalker,' she sniffs. 'I'm just an admirer, a genuine fan.'

'That's not the way it feels to me,' Daisy says.

To my amusement, big fat tears start rolling down Rosemary's cheeks.

'How does what Daisy's said make you feel?' I ask, leaning towards Rosemary.

'Like an idiot. Humiliated.'

Daisy softens. 'I'm sorry,' she says to Rosemary. 'It's just I'm under a lot of pressure and frankly I'm exhausted. I didn't mean to hurt you.'

I continue. 'Daisy is consumed with irrational fear, Rosemary, while you are dealing with unresolved grief. Both of these things started your problems with sleep and now they've become habitual. We need to break those thinking habits. Rosemary, what would you like to say to Daisy?'

'That I forgive you. I know you'd be happy for me to be part of your life, a bit like a godmother to your children. I mean things are so tough for you, working those long hours, your husband having his own business, I could be like a substitute mother to you, not that I want to impose myself, but I know you lost your own mother some years ago and perhaps I could fill a hole in your life and you could fill a hole in mine. And I could help you administer the Facebook group, be like your private secretary.'

'That's such a lovely idea, Rosemary,' I say, unable to keep a smile off my face.

Daisy's face goes from pale to bright red. 'Broccoli!' she says, standing up so abruptly, her chair topples backwards. 'Broccoli.'

And she walks straight out of my room.

I take a moment and then soften my voice. 'I'm sorry, Rosemary, but Daisy is very troubled. Her blog, her Facebook group, her journalism, they're just the outward face of her life and not a true reflection as to what is really going on in her world. You need to forgive her for her reactions. She doesn't mean to hurt you. Leave it with me and I'll have a word. I know that when she reflects on your kind offer, she'll welcome you with open arms. What a kind person you are, offering to help Daisy.'

'Thank you, Amity. I had no idea that Daisy was so troubled. She's very lucky that she's got you to help her.'

'And that she has you too,' I say with a broad smile. 'I think we'll call it a day.'

21

DAISY

What the hell was Amity doing, sharing things about me with that woman? Surely none of that was ethical and even if it was, she would need my consent, and I'm certainly not going to give it. I have no desire to have anything to do with Rosemary now or in the future. Doesn't Amity realise that Rosemary is like a stalker, trying to inveigle her way into my life? She's creepy and for all I know she's been sent by Aaron – although that doesn't seem very likely unless she's a relative. Oh goodness, what if she is?

I tell myself that I'm being ridiculous; that Rosemary is a sad, lonely person desperate to cling on to me while Amity is stepping over the mark with her therapy sessions. Perhaps Amity recruited Rosemary specifically to wind me up? But no, Rosemary would have to be a brilliant actress to pull that off. I think the woman is troubled and genuine. It's Amity who is most out of line here and the more I think about it, the more I'm sure that Amity is a charlatan.

I need a few minutes alone where I'm not going to be disturbed, so I nip into the ladies toilet on the therapy corridor and lock myself in a cubicle. I sit there for a few minutes trying to dissemble why I feel so claustrophobic around Rosemary. What is it about her that pushes all of my buttons? Despite my good night's sleep last night, my thoughts are still jumbled, so eventually I give up, wash my hands and walk up the stairs towards reception.

I'm lost in thought until I see Amity standing to one side of the dining room talking to an older man. He looks a lot like the chap I saw jogging along the beach early this morning, bald head, a paunchy stomach. He has his hand on Amity's shoulder and then he leans in to kiss her, a quick but gentle kiss on the lips. If the girl I saw with Amity was her daughter, then this white man cannot be the child's father. I'm curious to know more. Both Amity and the man disappear through the door that leads into the kitchen. I need to park my concerns over Rosemary and focus on Amity.

I turn around and wander into the living room where I perch on an armchair that has a view of the reception desk. When I see that Jenny is alone I walk over.

'Was that Amity's husband with her a few minutes ago?'

Jenny smiles. 'Yes. Keith is such a lovely man and very supportive of the spa.'

'I don't know how Amity does it all,' I say, remembering some of my journalistic interrogating skills. 'Running a business and a family with such a lovely daughter.'

'They have a son too, such a cute boy.'

'What's Keith's surname?' I ask, because if Amity is using his name for professional purposes then that might explain why I couldn't find her online.

'Smith,' Jenny says with a slight frown.

It's annoying that he has such a common surname, but even so, Amity is an unusual first name. If only I had access to the internet.

'Is there anything I can help you with?' Jenny asks.

'No, thanks, I'm just going to have a rest.'

BACK IN MY ROOM, I lie down on the bed and before I know it I've drifted off to sleep. When I wake up, the sun is shining on my face and I feel hot and a little disorientated. I force myself to come to and get out of bed, stretching and making my way to the window to let in some fresh air. As I glance down at the swimming pool, there's a man standing with his back to me, using some kind of vacuum cleaner to remove debris from the pool. There's something about him that makes me freeze, my hand on the window handle. And then he turns around.

It's him.

It's Aaron.

I take a step back and the room spins. I sink onto the side of the bed. It can't be Aaron, this is ridiculous, it must be my mind playing tricks just as Amity said.

I stand up again and walk cautiously back to the window. Pathetic as it is I whimper, because I am absolutely positive it is Aaron. He looks a little different now, his previously thick hair is balding and he's put on weight but it's definitely him. Did he follow me here? Has this all been some kind of set-up? As if he can sense my eyes on him, he turns around, looks up and stares at me, his cold, deep-set eyes unwavering, his lips set in a straight line. I edge backwards, hopeful that he can't see into my room, my heart hammering and my breath coming out as little gasps. Then he removes his phone from his pocket and dials a number, holding the phone up to his ear.

This can't be happening. I need to get out of here now; get in my car and drive far away. I should have followed my instincts yesterday.

I pull my clothes out of the wardrobe and get dressed in my jeans and a jumper. After flinging all my belongings into my suitcase, I do a cursory sweep of the room to double-check I haven't left anything behind, and then I pace to the door and turn the handle. Nothing happens. I try again, tugging at the door, making sure that it's really locked. It is. It's firmly closed. Have they locked me in? Has this been done on purpose?

My suitcase topples over as I dash to the bedside table and press the buzzer for reception. There's no answer. What the hell! I glance out of the window but there's no one by the pool now and no one walking along the beach. What should I do?

I look at the window. The section that opens isn't big enough for me to climb out of, and even if it was, there's no way I could jump from up here on the second floor to the terrace below without breaking my legs. Even if I *can* get out of the room, my car keys are locked away. I'll have to go on foot. I'll leave my suitcase and just take my handbag.

I press the reception button again and still there's no reply, and now the panic is mounting. I bang on the bedroom door with both fists and scream, 'Let me out! Someone let me out of here! I'm locked in!'

I don't know how long I'm banging on the door but my fists are sore and my voice is hoarse.

And then suddenly the door swings open and Amity is standing there.

'What's going on, Daisy? Why are you disturbing all of our other residents?'

'I was locked in and no one is answering when I ring the buzzer. I need to leave!'

I try to push past her but she's not budging from the door-way. 'Sit down, Daisy. Why are you behaving like this?'

'Because you're locking me in and Aaron is working here! I'm going home now!'

'I don't know what you're talking about. You're behaving irrationally, Daisy.' She walks into the room, closing it firmly behind her, pushing my suitcase to one side. 'Now let's sit down and I'll order you a cup of calming herbal tea.'

'You're not listening to me! Aaron is here. He was cleaning the swimming pool!' I'm pacing the room and I sound hysterical. I have to get out of this place. I'm fearful that Amity knows exactly what's happening, that perhaps this is all part of some big plan. 'Why is he here?' I jab my finger at her.

'Aaron is not cleaning the swimming pool. You're imagining things, Daisy.'

'Then who is? He was vacuuming just five minutes ago.'

'He's our new handyman and he's call Johnnie or something. I can assure you that he's not your Aaron.'

'I don't believe you! He saw me looking at him and he kept his eyes on me and took out his mobile phone.'

'Calm down, Daisy.'

'I'm not going to bloody calm down! I want you to tell me why he's here.'

I can see that Amity is getting annoyed now. Little red patches are blooming on her cheeks and she's clenching her jaw. Let her be angry; I certainly am.

'If you don't calm down immediately, Daisy, I'm going to have to call 999 and suggest you get sectioned.'

I open my mouth and no words come out. Instead, I sink onto the bed and stare at this woman. Is this what she planned all along, to make me look crazy? She's standing in front of the door, her arms crossed over her chest, her eyes slightly narrowed, staring at me. All her warmth from earlier has dissipated and now I only see coldness, hatred even.

'You got me here on purpose, didn't you?' I ask in a whisper, my fury turning to icy-cold fear. 'You know exactly who Aaron is. Why is that? What do you want from me, Amity?'

Amity's face is totally expressionless and that scares me even more.

'I have never met this Aaron. I don't know who he is and I can reassure you that he is not here.'

But I don't believe her. I don't trust this woman and all I know is that I need to get away from this place right now.

D aisy isn't making any sense. Well part of what she's surmising does, but the bit about Aaron is just confusing. I need to think.

I turn quickly and walk out of the door, slamming it behind me and then locking her in with my master key. I need time. Time to understand exactly what's going on here. It's possible that my hypnoses has made Daisy truly believe that Aaron is here and if Johnnie looks a little bit like Aaron, then she might put two and two together and make five. But that's unlikely. I may be a good therapist but I doubt I'm that good. No, it seems as if Daisy really is losing it and my interventions are working far better than I even dared hope.

As I walk back to my room, I take some slow, deep breaths and let the smile creep across my face. Daisy freaking out is truly wonderful and everything is panning out exactly as I hoped. This has been a long journey but oh my goodness, it's been worth the wait.

I've been looking for Daisy for years. Of course I didn't know who the journalist was for a very long time and I had next to nothing to go on. A year ago I decided to employ a private investigator called Jared Montfort, a chap that a friend used to find out more about the woman her husband was having an affair with. After a few months of research, he uncovered Daisy's name. It cost me a fortune, not that money is ever an issue as Keith makes sure I have more than enough. Bless him, he never questions what I spend it on either, but if he'd asked, I was going to say I bought a new piece of equipment for the spa.

'I've found what you want,' Jared Montfort said in his deep, heavy-smoker voice on the phone. 'Best come and meet me.'

I went to his run-down office in a back street in central Brighton. The door was unmarked and there was graffiti scribbled on the adjacent walls, so I rang the bell with trepidation. Jared Montfort is mid-fifties at a guess, ex-police – or so he says – with a heavy girth that makes Keith look positively fit. He ushered me through to a filthy office that stank of cigarette smoke and old takeaways. Such a disappointing stereotype, although none of that mattered when he talked me through what he'd found.

'It was a process of elimination. I went through every article that reported or commented on both of Kyle's murder trials, concentrating of course on the first one. That helped me compile a list of all the journalists who reported on it. Unfortunately there's no record of who actually sat in the public gallery in the courthouse and there are no recordings. Nevertheless, that helped me create a database of all the journalists assigned to court reporting. I compared that list of journalists to the list who covered Kyle's second trial. Most papers put the same journalist on both trials, unless they leave the paper or are promoted. That helped me whittle down the list to three journalists who could have been the source of the leak. I then arranged to meet Aaron Sullivan. You know about that.'

I nodded. Jared had rung me up about a month earlier saying that Aaron wanted twenty grand to share the journalist's name. I would have paid up but Jared was adamant I shouldn't. I guessed that was the ex-copper in him.

'I just saved you twenty grand,' he smiled wryly. 'I reckon it was a woman called Daisy McKenzie or Daisy Furness as she was called back then. She was young, twenty-three, and she'd reported on the first trial. But when the dates of the second trial were announced she quit her job. I interviewed her boss who said she was there one minute and gone the next, didn't even work out her notice. It was only with hindsight that the boss wondered whether she left to avoid reporting on the trial. And then it all made sense. It didn't take me long to find her. She'd changed her name when she got married and is now working for *Live Life London*, a London glossy magazine. She's got a blog called *Can't Sleep And Going Crazy* for insomniacs. It's very successful.'

And then I grinned because the plan came to me in an instant. I paid Jared the outstanding balance plus an extra fifteen per cent for doing such a good job and hurried out of his office. I went for a walk on the seafront and despite the vicious sea gusts, I sat down on a bench and found Daisy McKenzie's Facebook group. Using a fake name, I opened a Facebook account and joined the group. I wondered whether Daisy's guilt was giving her insomnia. I hoped so. And silently I thanked Daisy for making it so easy for me to find her. All I needed to do was create an insomnia programme for my new spa and invite her, the third-rate journalist, for a freebie and then she would be putty in my hands.

And so, here we are. As I sit in my chair and gaze out to sea, I think about Aaron. I didn't pay much attention to him back then. He was just the jury nobbler, not Leon's killer. Yes, he played a part, but my grief and anger skirted around him to focus on Kyle, the bastard who killed the love of my life, and the nameless, faceless journalist who was too much of a coward to speak up. Kyle was paying in prison on a life sentence, but the journalist – well she got away scot-free. I wonder about Aaron. How long was his prison sentence? Not that long I presume, so he would definitely be out of jail by now. I wonder what happened to him, where he is, what he's up to?

I turn on my laptop, go online and search for the case and specifically photos of Aaron Sullivan. I zoom in. Johnnie is almost bald and what little hair he has is shaven off whereas Aaron has a full head of hair and is slender. But that was over a decade ago and we all change with the passing of time.

'Oh my God,' I mutter aloud. The more I look at the photos the more I wonder if Daisy might be right. There is something about those deep-set, expressionless eyes that look familiar. Is it really possible that Johnnie could be Aaron? My stomach clenches at the thought. I don't pay much attention to members of the maintenance team, leaving the day-to-day running of this place to my manager, Carl, just thankful Keith was able to loan me helpers as and when required. But now I feel uneasy. Could Johnnie and Aaron be the same person? I telephone Keith who is still at home.

'Hi, love. I just wanted to ask a question about Johnnie. How long has he worked for you?'

'Johnnie? Do you mean Ronnie?'

'The chap who maintains the pool.'

'Yes, that's Ronnie. Why, what's he done?'

'Um, nothing. I was just wondering about him. How long has he worked for you?'

'What's up, Amity? I've got hundreds of people working for me so I can't possibly know much about them all. He's been around for a few years, I guess. Why?'

'Nothing. It's fine.'

'Has he done something wrong?'

'No, no. It's okay.'

'You're working too hard, love. Why don't we take the kids away for a long weekend? We could go to New York perhaps and you can do a spot of shopping. What do you think?'

'We can't just take them out of school, Keith. They're only allowed home for Saturday night.'

'Last time I checked I was paying for their education.' He sounds irritated.

'Come on, darling. You know what the law is. We'll only get the kids and us into trouble.'

'Let's talk later, okay?' And then he hangs up on me.

I think back through our brief conversation. There was something in the way Keith answered my question, the way he was trying to change the subject that piques my curiosity. It's like he was deflecting, not wanting to give me a straight answer about Johnnie or Ronnie, or whatever his name is. Does he genuinely not know much about the man? I think back to when Keith suggested I could use some of his team. Did we talk about Ronnie then? I doubt it because I was more interested in employing good therapists and chefs and focusing on the marketing. Might Ronnie be a nickname for Aaron? If so, then maybe Daisy isn't imagining things. Perhaps that man really is Aaron.

But Keith wouldn't employ an ex-convict, would he?

23

DAISY

I was up off the bed and racing towards the door, but I wasn't quick enough. Amity slipped out into the corridor and I could hear the lock click into place as she left. Who is this woman and what is she doing to me? I didn't even get the chance to tell her I need to leave and now I'm locked in this room yet again.

I walk back to the window and can see Aaron outside. He's kneeling by the side of the pool and doing something with a net. I can't look at him any more. What the hell should I do? Has this whole week been a set-up, designed to make me suffer? And why is Amity involved, what does she want from me? Then I see her walk out of the side door and stride towards Aaron. Their heads are close together and I can't see their expressions. Amity turns around and I quickly step away from the window so I can't be seen.

I try the door again but it's still locked. I pound my fists on it, even calling out for Rosemary, because despite everything, perhaps she might come to my rescue. But there's no answer and I suspect the soundproofing in this modern building is too good. I stride back to the bedside table and tug the drawer open, jamming my finger on the button there. To my surprise, a voice comes through the loud speaker.

'Hello, Jenny speaking. How can I help you?'

'I'm locked in my room and need to get out.'

'Oh dear, I'm sorry about that. I'll release the door now.'

I hear a click and race towards the door. To my utter relief, it's open. Did Amity not give instructions to Jenny to keep me locked in or is this a trick?

I creep out into the corridor, leaving the suitcase I packed earlier behind, because first I need to find my car keys and phone. Everything is quiet and the doors to the other guests" rooms are closed. It's a hell of a risk, but I wonder if I can get into Amity's office to look through her filing cabinet. I assume that's where she keeps her clients' notes and I need to see what she's written about me. I hear the clatter of crockery and cutlery coming from the dining room and realise the timing is perfect as the staff and guests will be tied up with lunch.

With my heart hammering in my chest, I walk along the therapy room corridor, past Doctor Dhingra's closed door and towards Amity's room. I knock gently on the door although I don't think she's there. When there's no answer I turn the door handle, and to my relief the door opens. I slip inside and head for her desk. Glancing over my shoulder first, I tug the drawer but as I expected, it's locked. I wonder if she keeps the key somewhere in this room.

There's a black hardback book on her desk which I open, a diary in fact. I flick through the pages. She only uses the first names of her clients and it doesn't disclose much to me. I turn then and walk to the door that I opened earlier. This is definitely a bedroom that Amity uses, the scent of her perfume hanging heavily in the air, an open wardrobe displaying a selection of linen outfits in neutral colours. Opposite the bed there's a desk and I see her handbag wedged underneath in the footwell. I bend down hoping to find keys or her phone. There's a pile of printed pages which I pull out, and to my utter dismay, realise they're photos of the pages I wrote in my journal – the journal she promised me would be private, that she would never read. I drop them back into the bag as if they're burning me. Now I am one hundred per cent certain that Amity wants something from me, that there's an agenda beyond helping cure my insomnia. But what? Why am I here?

I pull on the drop handle of a small drawer in the desk and to my surprise it opens. Inside is a pile of mobile phones. I rummage through them and almost cry with relief when I see mine, the turquoise background and grinning faces of Ollie and Millie peering up at me from my personalised phone case. I grab the phone and am just about to switch it on when the door swings open. I jump and shove the phone into the back pocket of my jeans, pulling down my jumper to hide the bulge. I feel sick with fear as the door opens wider, wondering how I'm going to explain why I'm here.

But it's not Amity. It's her daughter. My knees feel as if they're going to give way with relief as I grip the side of the desk.

'Hello. Who are you?' she asks.

'I'm waiting for Amity. Is she your mum?'

'Yeah.' She throws me a quizzical look reminiscent of her mother and it's as if this young, pretty girl on the cusp of womanhood can see straight into my head. She must know that I should be next door in the therapy room, not in her mother's private bedroom.

'What's your name?' I ask.

'Kitty,' she replies, but her voice is filled with suspicion. 'Are you ill? I'll go get my mum.'

'No, no. I'm fine,' I say, but Kitty has turned away and is speeding out of the room.

'Wait!' I say again, but it's too late. And now I know I have to get out of here because Kitty will tell her Mum and when Amity knows I've been snooping, I fear things will get so much worse.

Now I am sure that she and Aaron are in cahoots and she has lured me here under false pretences. There will be no article, no lovely review on Amity Augustiago's latest programme to cure sleeplessness and for a moment I even wonder if Garth was in collaboration with them too. But I quickly discount that. Garth just wanted a good article and for me to increase my productivity. I run now, darting out of the rooms, along the corridor and taking the stairs two steps at a time. I've got to get out of here because I'm sure that Amity wants me to suffer and that she and Aaron have been plotting this together.

Kitty is ambling along the upstairs corridor. Muttering a quick, 'Sorry,' I push past her and speed through the living room and into the front lobby where I run slap bang into Rosemary.

Her eyes are wide.

'What is it?' I snap. 'Are you in on this too? Did Aaron organise for you to come here, to needle your way into my life?'

'Daisy,' she steps in and puts a hand on my arm. I pull away from her. 'I know you're hurting. Is there anything I can do? Do you need a doctor?'

I realise then that she thinks I'm mad. This woman, who has such profound problems of her own, thinks that it's me who is the crazy one here.

'It's not me who needs the doctor. In fact, it's probably the police we need. There is something very wrong about this place and if I were you, I'd get out.'

'Oh, Daisy,' Rosemary says. 'You're such a brave person and I know you think I'm just a silly woman, a hanger-on, and perhaps I am. But I have such genuine respect for you and had no idea that you're struggling just like the rest of us. It makes me respect you even more.' She takes a step back and throws her hands up into the air. 'I'm going to leave you alone now because I can see I'm just making things worse, but please me know if you ever need any support, even if it's just someone to make you a cup of tea and then get out of your hair, I'd be happy to do that.' She blinks rapidly and turns around.

Suddenly I see Rosemary for who she really is. A lonely person who never got over her first love; a grieving soul who tries to latch on to anyone who might take her out of her own isolated bubble and give her the hope of some sort of a family, however remote that family might be. I'm just a means to an end for her. How could I have imagined that this woman had an agenda other than her own self-absorbed one? She's nothing more than a sad leech but she doesn't deserve my anger; rather she deserves my compassion and patience, neither of which I have time for right now.

'Rosemary, don't go,' I say. She turns around with an expression of surprise. 'I'm sorry, really sorry for being so horrible to you. I'll explain everything if I get out of here – when I get out of here. Send me a direct message. Oh, and I know you think I'm crazy but I promise you I'm not. I strongly suggest that you leave too.'

'What?' she exclaims.

My eyes dart around the white modern space. There's no one here except us. If I can just find my car keys, I can live without the rest of my belongings. I've got my phone so once I'm on the road I can call Haydn, and even the police if necessary. There must be an underground garage but it's not obvious how to get to it. I dart behind the reception desk and knock on the office door, but there's no answer and it's locked. And then I see a door to my left marked *Private*. It's set behind a large palm tree and I didn't notice it before. I yank the door open.

'Daisy!' Rosemary says, her voice laden with concern. I feel bad but I have to ignore her. I let the door close with a gentle thud behind me and I find myself in a cool, concrete corridor with concrete steps running downwards. I hurtle down them and pull open another heavy door and find myself in a cavernous, underground garage. An automatic light comes on which startles me. The air feels cold down here as if this space is forgotten, although there's a heavy smell of diesel. There are about twelve parked cars and mine is adjacent to the far wall, but what good is that without the key? I don't know how to break into a car or start it without one. What am I going to do?

24

I stride towards the pool where I can see Ronnie crouching to one side fiddling with some equipment.

'Should I call you Ronnie or Aaron?' I say through gritted teeth, my arms crossed over my chest.

'Call me whatever you like, luv,' he says without looking up.

'I'm not your love. I'm your employer.'

'Last time I checked, I was on your hubby's books. What's the problem, anyway? I'm just doing my job cleaning the pool.' He stands up slowly, wiping his wet hands on his jeans and then fixes his eyes on me, causing a shiver of recognition.

'How long have you worked for Keith?' I say, my voice barely audible.

'Long enough.'

'Are you Aaron? Were you convicted for jury influencing? Is Ronnie short for Aaron?'

'What's with all the questions, Amity?'

'Does my husband know who you are? That you've got a criminal record?'

'Best ask him that yourself, luv.'

'He's not here and you are. Please answer.'

'Look, your husband is loyal to his employees. I aint going to say a word out of line.'

'I'm not asking you to,' I say.

'You've been married to Keith for...what is it?' He scratches his chin and looks up at the grey sky. 'Must be coming up fourteen years now, yet you still don't have a clue what's going on, do you?'

'What are you talking about?' I whisper. 'Just tell me, is Kyle your cousin? Were you convicted of jury tampering?'

He just grins at me as if this is the most hilarious thing he's ever heard and then he lets out a snort, turns around and strides away.

'Wait!' I shout, but he doesn't look back and my voice gets carried away by the strong sea breeze.

I don't understand what's going on here. Why is Keith employing Aaron? Or has Aaron got himself employed here to keep an eye on Daisy. But if so why? And how did he know that Daisy was going to be staying here?

I try to recall when Aaron first started cleaning the pool. It wasn't long ago and perhaps he somehow intercepted Daisy's emails or phone messages and discovered she was going to be staying at my spa. I try to look at this from another angle. Perhaps it's a good thing that Aaron is here, contributing to Daisy's sense of paranoia; he's actually helping my cause. In fact better than that, perhaps I can set things up to make Daisy's death appear as if Aaron did it, or at least he pushed her to take her own life. That would be much more satisfactory all around. From the way he spoke, he confirmed what Keith said, that my husband has employed him for a while. Whatever is going on it feels as if things are slipping out of my control just when the finishing line is in sight.

I shiver because the air has turned damp and cold and

then I glance at my watch. I need to get back to Daisy because she's been locked in for a while and I don't want her to create a racket and disturb my other guests. Hurrying back into the building, I stride along the guest corridor and slide my master key into her door, my heart beating hard with anticipation.

'Daisy,' I say, as I open the door. Her suitcase is lying on its side and her bag is dumped on a chair but the room is empty.

'Daisy!' I repeat as I hurry into the bathroom. It's also empty. How the hell did she get out? Did one of my numpty staff let her go? Fury and fear curdle in my stomach as I race out of her room and run back down the corridor towards the office. She could bring my whole business crashing down if I don't get to her before she leaves.

I can hear soft voices and the clatter of cutlery coming from the dining room, where I assume my other guests are being attended to by our well-trained staff. Jenny isn't behind the reception desk or in the office, but perhaps that's just as well. With trembling fingers, I bring up the live images on the office computer from our numerous CCTV cameras, and scour each box eagerly looking for Daisy. It's not possible for her to leave the premises, not without a key, and I know Jenny would never do anything so stupid as to let her go without my permission. I straighten up and punch in the numbers into the wall safe where we keep all of the car keys and to my relief I see the keys to Daisy's Golf are still here. I jam the safe shut again and then peer at the computer screen again. Bingo.

There's movement in the underground garage. The stupid woman is crouched beside a car. What is she doing there? A horrible thought crosses my mind. Does Daisy have a spare car key with her, a key that I didn't spot when I went through her belongings?

I race out of the office and wrench the door open to the

basement staircase, then run down the concrete steps. It's only when I stand at the bottom that I take a deep breath and try to compose myself. It's dark down here, lit just by some security lights, the main strip lights coming on from movement sensors. I open the door into the garage and stand still for a moment. I can't see Daisy, but a moment ago she was crouching between her car and the adjacent BMW. I stride towards her Golf.

'Daisy, I know you're here. We need to talk.' My voice echoes slightly in this large concrete box, a box that cost an absolute fortune to build but was a vital necessity for the spa.

Her head pops up and she starts to run.

'There's nowhere to go, Daisy. You can't get out of here. Besides, I'm not the enemy, I just want to help you.' That's not strictly true of course but I'm hardly going to show my true colours this late in our game.

Daisy stands on the far side of her car. 'Why are you employing Aaron?'

I debate continuing the charade of pretending that Aaron is a figment of her imagination but decide there's no point any longer. I can be truthful. 'I don't know why he's here. It's as much a mystery to me as it is to you. I just know him as Johnnie, the pool cleaner.'

'I saw you talking to him. What did he say?'

'I asked him to confirm his identity.'

'And did he?'

'To a point.'

'Who are you really, Amity? And what do you have to do with Kyle and Aaron, because I know you're involved somehow. It's no coincidence that I'm here, is it?'

Oh, Daisy, you're cleverer than I thought.

I sigh. 'No, it's not a coincidence. I was Leon's partner, his fiancée. We were planning a life together and I was pregnant with his child when he was brutally murdered. I loved him and his death was devastating to me.'

'That's not true. Leon was married to Debra.'

'I know Leon was married.' I sigh again. 'But they were divorcing and he was going to marry me.'

'That never came out in the press.'

'Of course it didn't. Debra milked the grieving widow role as best she could. It wouldn't have looked good for the world to know that Leon was in love with someone else, that I was pregnant with his child.' I spit out the words.

'Did you lure me here on purpose? What do you want from me?'

I can see her trembling and that at least brings me some consolation. I'm grateful that I can think on my feet so quickly because immediately a new plan formulates in my mind. I'll tell her the truth; I'll tell her that I did bring her here to find out more about her and to increase her suffering. Because now I have a wonderful opportunity for blackmail.

'I want you to suffer, Daisy, because you didn't tell the truth. If you'd exposed the fact that Aaron and Kyle were jury nobbling then Kyle would have been convicted and he wouldn't have gone on to murder the love of my life. If you had told the truth, then Leon wouldn't have died.'

I can see the shock on her face; the shock that I know her filthy secret, that she is a coward lacking all principles.

'What do you want from me?' she asks lamely. 'Was your aim to make my insomnia worse? And what about the review?'

'Your sleeplessness was going to improve but I wanted to make the process of getting there so painful. As for the review, you'd never write the truth though, would you? You're too worried about your secret getting out.'

'Why is Aaron here?'

'He works for Keith and has nothing to do with me.'

I can tell from Daisy's face that she's sceptical, which is ironic because it really is the truth.

'Didn't you recognise him from the trial?' she asks.

I shake my head. I'm not going to tell Daisy that I had a breakdown after Leon's death, that I barely made it through each day knowing my fiancé's baby was growing inside me, knowing I'd have to go through her birth all alone, knowing she would never meet her father, knowing that legally, Leon died married to another woman. It was Keith who scooped me up a mere month before Kitty was born, who held me as I sobbed and quivered with fear, who told me that he would care for me and my newborn. When the trial happened, it was Keith who attended every day, because how could I go there with a newborn? He was my protector in every sense: emotional, physical and financial. When Aaron's trial took place, Keith whisked me and Kitty away to southern Spain where he has a villa and we only returned once both Aaron and Kyle were locked away in prison. So no, I never saw Aaron in the flesh, and frankly I wasn't that interested in him. It was Kyle who killed Leon; it was Kyle who inhabited my nightmares for so many years. Besides, these days Aaron looks very different. The only strange thing is why is he here, working for Keith? Is he here specifically for Daisy and if so, why?

We're both startled as the garage door starts opening with a grinding sound, lifting upwards towards the ceiling. To my surprise, it's Keith in his navy Bentley driving rather too fast.

Daisy spots her opportunity and darts through the parked cars towards the exit but Keith sees her and swerves the car towards her. The tyres screech as he comes to a sudden halt just millimetres from Daisy, who has frozen in shock. The garage door starts coming down again behind him, a grinding sound that's almost deafening. Daisy steps to the side of the car, no doubt trying to dash under the garage door before it's too late, but Keith swings his car door open and blocks her way. I can't understand why Keith is stopping Daisy. How does he know that I don't want her to run away, that she's here because I want her to suffer?

The shutter door comes to a halt with a shudder and Daisy is standing in front of Keith, her eyes wide, her face ghostly white.

'What's going on?' Keith asks, leaning his elbows on the top of his car door, totally nonchalant as if it's perfectly normal to drive at someone and then block their way.

'Why are you here?' I ask. 'I thought you were in London today.'

'More to the point, what is *she* doing here?' He glowers at Daisy; this isn't making any sense to me. He points at her and says, 'You must have thought you were so clever, working out that Amity was Leon's fiancée, checking yourself into her spa. What were you going to do to her? Were you going to harm her or were you just going to write a terrible review?'

What on earth is Keith talking about? How does he even know who Daisy is?

I stare at my husband, shocked at how his eyes are narrowed and his lips are pulled back, as if he's baring his teeth. What is going on here?

'What?!' Daisy exclaims. 'I'm just here to cure my insomnia. Amity found me, she invited me, not the other way around.' I can see that Daisy is riddled with panic, her eyes darting all over the place, as if she's desperately seeking a way out of here. There is no exit. This is a concrete box and the only way the garage door will open is with a remote control or through the main control switchboard in the office.

'How do you know who Daisy is?' I ask Keith as my brain slowly starts to crunch into action.

'I've always known and when Aaron rang me a few

minutes ago to say that Daisy was here and you were asking lots of questions, I knew I had to sort things.'

'So Johnnie is Aaron?' I ask quietly.

Keith nods.

'Did you hire him?' I ask.

Keith shrugs his shoulders and I realise with horror that I don't know my husband at all. 'Did you hire Kyle too?' I ask, my voice sounding unnaturally shrill.

He just curls his lips, totally nonchalant, but something flips inside me. 'Tell me!'

'Everything I do is to protect you, my love.' He moves as if to pat my arm but I pull away from him.

'Tell me the truth,' I demand.

'Not in front of her.' Keith inclines his head towards Daisy. 'You should never trust a journalist.'

25

I'm not sure whether it's terror that's causing my brain fog or if I really am confused. It's so strange that Amity doesn't seem to know what's going on. Why is she staring at her husband like that? Why is she asking questions about Aaron?

And then it clicks. Keith knows.

He must be involved in everything, all of the past and the present. But how? If Keith is Aaron's employer, then he probably put Aaron up to everything. Aaron might just be Keith's minion, the person who does his dirty work. If Keith is pulling the strings, then he might be behind the blackmail, and that makes him the person who might expose how I took his bribe and how I didn't speak up when I discovered the jury nobbling – because why would Aaron have five grand in cash to give to me? It makes sense that Aaron was just doing his boss's dirty work. Perhaps Keith now wants to get rid of me because no normal person would drive their car at a pedestrian.

There is no way out. Am I in mortal danger? Could Amity be in danger too? Surely not. It's obvious how much Keith adores his wife but she's looking at him through narrowed eyes as if he's a stranger. I have to do something. I need to dig deep and remember how I used to be when I was a young and resourceful journalist.

While Keith and Amity are staring at each other, I reach into my back pocket and take out my mobile phone. I daren't look down to see if I've got a signal and I know the chances are slim, because we're underground in a concrete box, but I need to try. I just pray that it won't let out a beep when I switch it on, so I press the volume down button at the same time as the on button, glancing at it as little as possible, keeping my eyes on Keith and Amity. The phone vibrates slightly in my hand and Keith's head swings towards me.

But then Amity says, 'Did you hire Kyle?'

I feel for the power button on my iPhone and press the start button rapidly five times, just praying that the phone doesn't emit any beeps. I then glance down and press the loudspeaker button, my hands shaking so much it makes it difficult to slip the phone back into my jeans pocket. I pray that there is reception and turn my attention to Keith and Amity.

'Did you hire Kyle?' she asks again. 'Answer me, Keith!' She's moved to the side of his car now and is gripping his wrist. 'Did you have something to do with Leon's death?' She's sobbing, almost hysterical, and for a moment I feel the pressure lift from me.

I take a few steps backwards but Keith sees me and swings around, pointing his finger at me.

'Don't move!' he says in a voice that sends shivers through me.

I just stand there as if my feet are glued to the concrete floor, knowing I'm going to have to wait for an opportunity to make a dash for the door. In that split second Keith leans into his car, and then he's standing behind the car door, his feet planted apart, pointing a gun at me.

A gun. I've never even seen one except on television. Amity looks equally horrified, her eyes large, her jaw slack.

'What are you doing, Keith?' she yelps. 'Why have you got a gun?'

'Oh, Amity,' he says, his voice hard and mocking, his eyes never wavering from me. 'You always thought Leon was your perfect man, the good guy, but he wasn't. He was on the fiddle, supplying my network with prescription drugs. Didn't he tell you he was about to be interviewed by the police, that he would have lost his doctor's licence, that he was about to expose my lucrative business? Did you really believe he was going to leave Debra to be with you? He was never going to divorce her; he needed her parents' money.'

'What?' She staggers back and hits a red car.

'Leon had to go. I hoped I would never have to tell you this, Amity, but yes, Leon had to be disposed of.'

'But what about me?' Her voice cracks.

He chuckles, which is at odds with this horrifying situation and the fact he still has his gun pointed at me. 'You were just a bonus, love.'

A strange noise comes from Amity – a bit like a strangling sound. ''It's not too late for you and me, Amity, and we need to think about Jaxton. But it's too late for Daisy. When people open their big mouths they have to be taken care of. This woman is a journalist so she's never going to keep her trap shut.'

Instinct kicks in and I duck down behind a car.

'The police are on their way!' I yell, desperately hoping that's true, and that I have sufficient signal for the emergency services to hear everything that is being said. Immediately a shot rings out and instinctively, I throw myself onto the ground where I can see straight through the undersides of two parked cars. To my horror, Amity lunges at her husband and the gun flies out of Keith's hand, skidding across the concrete floor, under the first car. I need to get to it, but how? Without thinking, I scramble underneath the first car, a 4x4 with enough space for me to crawl under easily. I can see that Keith is reaching under the other car, a red sports car, to get the gun, but he's much bigger than me and there's insufficient space for him to haul himself under it. Our eyes meet and I see a terrifying hardness in his.

He jumps up and levers himself down again so that his legs are extended under the car, but I'm quicker and smaller and I grab the gun just as his booted foot comes towards me.

I yelp as I crawl backwards, catching the back of my head on the underbelly of the car. My head pounds but I ignore the pain. My fingers are clasped around the gun and, quickly, I edge out from under the car, standing up. The red sports car is between us now. With trembling hands I point the gun straight at Keith.

It's as if Amity doesn't see me because she tugs at Keith's arm.

'You need to tell me,' she yells, her face contorted with confusion and fear.

'Aaron!' Keith shouts and my heart sinks, because if Aaron turns up, then it's certainly all over for me.

'Why was Leon working for you?' Amity begs. 'I don't understand.'

But I do. Now everything slots into place. Perhaps Amity didn't realise that Kyle killed Jason over some gang warfare, that the selling of illegal drugs was involved and that Kyle was taking revenge.

'Are you a drugs gang boss, Keith?' I ask. 'Is that how you have so much money?'

'Shut your mouth,' he growls, his eyes fixed on the barrel of the gun.

'I thought you had a property and logistics empire,' Amity says. Her voice is weak now.

'You like spending the dosh, don't you, love?' he says to her. 'It's not easy to make the amounts that we're raking in without bending the rules once in a while.'

I take advantage of Keith talking to Amity and put my finger on the trigger, the gun still pointed at Keith. I'm shocked at how calm I feel. 'But it's not just the odd rule, is it, Keith? Your logistics empire is founded on distributing illegal drugs and that's why you employed Kyle and why you employ Aaron. They're your minions, except Kyle wasn't very good at his job, was he, getting caught twice over? And Leon was just a small cog in your big wheel.'

'Not Leon!' Amity moans.

'He needed money, did your perfect man,' Keith says with a sneer. 'Trying to divorce his first wife, you with a baby on the way expecting to be supported. You're expensive, my love, aren't you? I told the boys, hone in on the doctors and nurses with problems in their personal lives. They're the ones that need the cash, that are easy prey. Leon was weak. But then he threatened to tell the police everything. If he'd opened his trap, the whole network could have come tumbling down.'

'No!' Amity sobs.

It's as if Keith has temporarily forgotten that I'm here because he's putting his arms around Amity now, even though she's trying to push him away.

'Amity, get over here!' I shout.

'No you bloody don't!' Keith says, holding her tightly. 'Aaron!' he bellows again.

We all freeze as the door I walked in through opens with a creak. I swing round, pointing the gun at the doorway, realising that Keith will probably start racing towards me. In that split second, I ready myself for Aaron and the reality that he'll be a much better shot than me.

'What the hell!' Rosemary exclaims, her jaw dropping open. 'I heard shouts.'

I swing back towards Keith but it's too late; he's rushing around the car towards me.

I pull the trigger.

26

Can't Sleep And Going Crazy

Public Group. 243K members. 10+ posts a day.

Pinned Post by Daisy McKenzie
Many of you will have read the reports in the papers about the sudden closing down of The Serinity Spa. Some of you may have realised that the abrupt closure came immediately after my stay there. I will in due course be making public the exact details of what happened, including both the conventional and unconventional (and unethical) methods that Amity Augustiago used. But for now, suffice it to say – and no thanks to Amity – my insomnia has been cured. I have been sleeping between five and eight hours every night for the past week. I'm going to be temporarily closing this Facebook group. I'll be back with more information as soon as I can. In the meantime, thank you all for your support and I wish you a peaceful and restful sleep. Daisy x

Rosemary Burgh
I'm with you all the way, lovely Daisy. Xxx

R osemary posts her comment within seconds of me writing the post, pinning it to the top of the page before I have the chance to turn off commenting. I recall how I might have thought her comment sycophantic before, but now I just smile at it and wonder whether Rosemary's insomnia has improved.

It's a few weeks later and I'm walking out of the cavernous reception area of the very newspaper where I started my journalism career all those years ago. They moved offices since then and this place is quite the upgrade with all its marble and glass. Last week, I had an interview with their head of human resources and today I returned for a chat with the editor, Nat Golding. The crazy thing is they approached me and asked if I'd consider writing for them as a features writer. I didn't need long to think about that.

'I was very impressed with your article about The Serinity Spa and Amity Augustiago. You've got a good nose for a story,' Nat Golding said. 'How would two days in the office and the rest working from home sound to you? We need some fresh blood in our features section.'

I managed to negotiate a salary considerably greater than what I'm earning at *Live Life London* and I'll be starting in a fortnight's time, so it's hardly surprising that I'm walking out onto this London street as if I'm dancing on air.

. . .

IT ALL KICKED off after I wrote the promised article about The Serinity Spa. It was too important an article for *Live Life London*, so Garth very kindly suggested I pitch it as a freelance piece. There I was, so desperate to make the big time, to have the lead article in a major paper, and then I was handed a story that is going global. I can see Netflix commissioning a series about Amity's life but I'm getting ahead of myself.

I think back to that fateful day when I shot Keith. Fortunately for all of us, and particularly him, I was a terrible shot, and because Keith was running I missed, but the bullet ricocheted off the side of a Mercedes and tore into the back of Keith's knee causing him to collapse and cry out with pain. Both Amity and I were in such shock. I dropped the gun and Amity froze. It was Rosemary who took control and who opened the garage door, just as the police sirens wailed signalling their arrival.

The focus of my article wasn't Keith but Amity. I listed all the unconventional and unethical methods that she used in her false mission to cure my insomnia, but what I couldn't escape from were the conventional methods. With hindsight, I can see that Amity is probably a good therapist. A lot of what she was doing was grounded in methods that have been proven to work but she twisted things. I'll never know exactly what she said when she put me into a hypnotic trance but I do know that blasting me with music, controlling the lights and locking me in my room was illegal, unethical and in contravention of everything a therapist is permitted to do. I may have thought that I was crazy but in many ways it is Amity who is the craziest of us all.

She might have wanted to cause me harm but was she really the villain? No. She was a victim. First of all she lost Leon, the man she truly thought was the love of her life, and then she was swept up by Keith. How she never realised that he was the mastermind behind a massive, global criminal network of drug traffickers and that he laundered his money through his commercial properties, I really don't know. Perhaps she was so swept away by his money and the luxury lifestyle he gave her that she refused to really look. I would not describe Amity as naive, but maybe she was. The one truth in this story is I believe Keith really loved Amity and although I doubt she loved him with the same passion, she certainly cared for him.

Keith is in a maximum security jail now, on remand without bail and his trial is expected to be held at The Old Bailey. I think I might attend it. The police hailed me the hero for bringing his empire crumbling down, yet I wasn't any great mastermind. Sometimes it's just a matter of being in the right place at the right time.

Amity has lost everything. It's rumoured that the spa is up for sale and as it was in her name only, I assume she will be well rewarded for that. Apparently she and the kids have relocated to California, but frankly I don't care. As for Aaron, the man who haunted my days and came to life in my nightmares, I've no idea where he has gone. With his paymaster behind bars, I realise I have nothing left to fear.

Despite all of the introspection, it was Haydn who helped me see the light.

The evening I returned home, with Margot despatched to her house and the children tucked up in bed, we sat down and I told him everything. I explained how I failed to tell the authorities about the jury nobbling, how I accepted the bribe and how I lived with the regret of not speaking up, and that Leon's murder has been on my conscience for all of these years. Haydn wasn't angry, he wasn't shocked, I think he was just genuinely sad that I didn't feel able to tell him the truth and that it affected my health and wellbeing to such an extent.

'Ultimately it would be his word against yours, Daisy, and what exactly did you do wrong? You accepted a bribe, except no one can ever prove that's what happened. The police are never going to believe a convicted criminal over you, a respected journalist and the person who exposed a massive drugs network. It's thanks to you they caught Keith and destroyed his global business.' He took my hands and gazed into my eyes. 'I don't want you to ever keep something from me like that again. Do you promise?'

'Yes,' I said. 'And I hope I never get myself into a mess like that again.'

BUT THAT'S all in the past now and as of today, I have an extremely exciting future.

I turn left onto a busy London street just as my phone rings and Haydn's number flashes up.

'I got it!' I say, in an excited whisper. 'And we won't need to worry about money.' I try not to think about the fact I'll have to work so much harder than I did at *Live Life London*. I can't see Nat allowing me any slack like Garth did. But hopefully that'll be fine because I'm sleeping so much better now, which means I can concentrate, I can be productive. And I'll be working from home much of the week, so I'll still be there for the children.

'Congratulations! I'm so proud of you, Daisy,' Haydn says. I can hear the smile in his voice. 'Let's go to a restaurant tonight and order a bottle of champagne to celebrate. I'll get Mum over to babysit.'

I stop on the pavement and a besuited man curses under his breath as he steps to the side to avoid me.

'No, Haydn. Our marriage deserves the time and space for us to be a couple. It's not a threesome with your mother. I'm done with her snide remarks and her lack of support for my career. Besides, we'll be able to afford a babysitter now.'

There's a beat of silence before Haydn answers. 'You're right. Just the two of us. I'll see you later, darling.'

A LETTER FROM MIRANDA

Thank you very much for reading The Insomniac.

I'm going to let you into a secret! Sleep and I have a challenging relationship. I could blame my inability to stay asleep on pain, as my leg frequently wakes me up in the night, but the truth is, I've never experienced easy sleep. I'm a very light sleeper and I have extremely vivid dreams. So much so, that a few weeks ago, I dreamed a complete plot for a book and remember waking momentarily at some unearthly hour, pleased with myself that I had my next book planned. When I awoke in the morning, I couldn't remember any of the detail! If there's anyone in need of a stay in a sleep clinic, it's me. Unfortunately, by writing this book, I've just scared myself silly and don't think that'll be happening any time soon!

This novel is totally a product of my imagination, and I apologise sincerely if I have made any mistakes regarding hypnosis or other therapies. All the hypnotherapists I have met (including my wonderful late uncle) work to the very highest standards and are nothing like fictional Amity. Indeed, I am a great advocate of hypnosis, journal writing, meditation and the other therapies I've mentioned in this book, and there's nothing better than having a wonderful soak in a floatation tank.

Once again, a huge thank you to my amazing editor Jan Smith, who steers me through the plotting conundrums and makes sure that my act breaks and mid-point turns occur when they're meant to. The writing process with the Inkubator Books team is collaborative and extraordinarily supportive. A very big thank you to Brian Lynch, Garret Ryan, Stephen, Claire, Sheila and the rest of the team. You have made my writing dreams come true.

I would also like to thank the book blogging community who so generously review my books, do cover reveals and share their thoughts with readers. A huge thank you to Carrie Shields (@carriereadsthem_all) and Zooloos Book Tours.

Lastly but most importantly, thank *you* for reading my books. I love to chat with readers via BookBub, Goodreads or Instagram so please reach out and say hello. Reviews on Amazon and Goodreads help other people discover my novels, so if you could spend a moment writing an honest review, no matter how short it is, I would be massively grateful.

My warmest wishes,

Miranda

www.mirandarijks.com

ALSO BY MIRANDA RIJKS

THE VISITORS

(A Psychological Thriller)

I WANT YOU GONE

(A Psychological Thriller)

DESERVE TO DIE

(A Psychological Thriller)

YOU ARE MINE

(A Psychological Thriller)

ROSES ARE RED

(A Psychological Thriller)

THE ARRANGEMENT

(A Psychological Thriller)

THE INFLUENCER

(A Psychological Thriller)

WHAT SHE KNEW

(A Psychological Thriller)

THE ONLY CHILD

(A Psychological Thriller)

THE NEW NEIGHBOUR

(A Psychological Thriller)

THE SECOND WIFE

(A Psychological Thriller)

THE INSOMNIAC

(A Psychological Thriller)

FATAL FORTUNE

(Book 1 in the Dr Pippa Durrant Mystery Series)

FATAL FLOWERS

(Book 2 in the Dr Pippa Durrant Mystery Series)

FATAL FINALE

(Book 3 in the Dr Pippa Durrant Mystery Series)